– The –
Drummer Boy's Battle

Trailblazer Books

TITLE	HISTORIC CHARACTERS
Abandoned on the Wild Frontier	Peter Cartwright
Attack in the Rye Grass	Marcus and Narcissa Whitman
The Bandit of Ashley Downs	George Müller
The Betrayer's Fortune	Menno Simons
The Chimney Sweep's Ransom	John Wesley
Danger on the Flying Trapeze	Dwight L. Moody
The Drummer Boy's Battle	Florence Nightingale
Escape from the Slave Traders	David Livingstone
Flight of the Fugitives	Gladys Aylward
The Hidden Jewel	Amy Carmichael
Imprisoned in the Golden City	Adoniram and Ann Judson
Kidnapped by River Rats	William and Catherine Booth
Listen for the Whippoorwill	Harriet Tubman
The Queen's Smuggler	William Tyndale
Quest for the Lost Prince	Samuel Morris
The Runaway's Revenge	John Newton
Shanghaied to China	Hudson Taylor
Spy for the Night Riders	Martin Luther
The Thieves of Tyburn Square	Elizabeth Fry
Traitor in the Tower	John Bunyan
Trial by Poison	Mary Slessor
The Warrior's Challenge	David Zeisberger (The Moravians)

– The –
Drummer Boy's Battle

Dave & Neta Jackson

Illustrated by Julian Jackson

BETHANY HOUSE PUBLISHERS
MINNEAPOLIS, MINNESOTA 55438

Published by Bethany House Publishers
A Ministry of Bethany Fellowship, Inc.
11300 Hampshire Avenue South
Minneapolis, Minnesota 55438

Printed in the United States of America.

Library of Congress Cataloging-in-Publication Data

Jackson, Dave.
    The drummer boy's battle : Florence Nightingale / Dave and Neta Jackson ; text illustrations by Julian Jackson.
        p.   cm. — (Trailblazer books ; #21)
    Includes bibliographical references (p.).
    Summary: In 1854, after being wounded while serving as a drummer in the British army in the Crimean War, twelve-year-old Robbie Robinson is cared for by Florence Nightingale and becomes involved in her efforts to improve the medical care of the sick and wounded soldiers.
    ISBN 1–55661–740–2
    1. Nightingale, Florence, 1820–1910—Juvenile fiction.
2. Crimean War, 1853–1856—Juvenile fiction. [1. Nightingale, Florence, 1820–1910—Fiction. 2. Crimean War, 1853–1856—Fiction. 3. Nurses—Fiction. 4. Christian life—Fiction. I. Jackson, Neta. II. Jackson, Julian, ill. III. Title.] IV. Series: Jackson, Dave. Trailblazer books ; #21.
PZ7.J132418Dr   1996
[Fic]—dc21   96–45855
                                           CIP
                                           AC

Robbie Robinson is based on a real character, a drummer boy for the Sixty-Eighth Light Infantry who lost his hand at the Battle of Alma. He described himself as "Miss Nightingale's man," and he vowed to devote his "civil and military career to Miss Nightingale." He carried her letters and messages, escorted her when she went from the Barracks Hospital to the General Hospital, and had charge of the lamp she carried at night. Later in life, Mr. Robinson wrote his memoirs, which are with the Florence Nightingale exhibit in the British Museum.

However, the account of Robbie's family, his brother Peter, and their interaction with the Nightingale family before the Crimean War are fictional.

Most of the other characters in this story are historical (including William Jones and Peter Grillage). But, in order to simplify the story, many other historical characters have been left out, focusing only on a few to help tell the basic story of Florence Nightingale and her role in the Crimean War.

DAVE AND NETA JACKSON are a husband/wife writing team who have authored or coauthored many books on marriage and family, the church, and relationships, including the books accompanying the Secret Adventures video series, the Pet Parables series, the Caring Parent series, and the newly released *Hero Tales*.

The Jacksons have two married children: Julian, the illustrator for TRAILBLAZER BOOKS, and Rachel, who has recently blessed them with a granddaughter, Havah Noelle. Dave and Neta make their home in Evanston, Illinois, where they are active members of Reba Place Church.

CONTENTS

Chapter 1

Party at the Big House

ROBBIE KNEW SOMETHING WAS WRONG when he saw his older sister, Margo, sitting on the stoop in the twilight holding baby Mae, her face streaked with tears. Sissy and Tommy, who were five and seven, crowded close to her skirts.

"Is it...Papa?" Robbie asked, his mouth dry.

Ten-year-old Robbie had been out all day, taking old Mrs. Dobble's brown cow to graze along the road. When he brought the cow back at dusk, the toothless old lady had paid him with a tin of milk—fresh, warm milk for baby Mae and Sissy and Tommy. He had imagined how pleased Mama would be—but now the pail hung from his hand, forgotten.

Margo nodded wordlessly. Then Robbie heard it: the sound of their father inside the shabby cottage retching again and again—those horrible dry heaves, with nothing coming up—and then a long groan.

Margo, who was fourteen, buried her face in baby Mae's cotton gown, while Sissy stuck her thumb in her mouth and Tommy looked ready to cry. Their father was sick—had been ever since he and Peter had come home from London two nights ago. Thomas Robinson was a "carter"—hiring himself and his mule cart out to do hauling jobs—but work was hard to find around the little village of Wellow. So the first week of June that summer of 1852, he and sixteen-year-old Peter had harnessed Cinder the mule and gone to London to find work.

They'd been gone three weeks. "No news is good news," Sally Robinson had said each day. "Maybe they found work and can't get away." But each evening she had stood in the doorway and, shielding her eyes from the low-hanging sun, looked down the road, hoping to see her men coming home.

Then, two nights ago, they'd seen the mule and cart coming. But as it came closer they could only see Peter sitting on the narrow driver's seat of the four-wheeled cart. Where was Papa? But as Cinder turned into the narrow dirt driveway which went around the little cottage to the mule shed in the rear, they saw Thomas half sitting, half lying in the cart box.

Mama and Peter had helped Papa into the house and put him to bed. Peter said he and Papa had found work carting away rubble from a warehouse that had burned down. But the pub where they found lodging was crowded and foul smelling, and many people were getting sick with vomiting and diarrhea. And then Papa...

That was two days ago, and now Papa was worse. Robbie handed the pail of milk to Margo and crept quietly into the cottage. Papa was groaning on the bed half-hidden behind a quilt hung for a curtain. Mama barely glanced up from wringing out a damp cloth and trying to moisten his dry lips.

"Robbie! Run up to the Embley estate and ask the young Miss Nightingale to come," she said.

Robbie swallowed. He'd never been up to the fancy house by himself before. "Why can't Peter—?"

"Peter took Cinder out looking for work—at least that's where he's supposed to be!" Sally Robinson snapped. "Get along now—Papa needs help fast."

Robbie ran out the door, past the weepy knot of his three sisters and little brother outside their thatch-roofed cottage, and took off down the road toward Embley. The Robinsons lived on the edge of the vast Nightingale estate, and sometimes Papa did jobs there, like when they added that big wing with more bedrooms for guests and a large hall for parties. Peter had a way with horses, so every now and then he helped out the stable man there. But the Nightingales only lived at Embley half the year. The muggy summer months were spent up north at Lea Hurst, their summer home.

As Robbie's feet pounded the hard-packed dirt, he realized he hadn't had any supper. His stomach pinched with hunger. But there would be no supper until he brought Miss Nightingale back with him.

As the wiry boy approached the main gate of the Embley driveway, he saw the curving drive was filled with carriages and teams of sleek, matched pairs of horses. Grooms leaned against their masters' carriages, smoking pipes or polishing the brass lamps. More carriages were arriving and pulling up to the front door, letting out laughing ladies in swishing gowns accompanied by gentlemen in tall hats. The great house was alight, each window sparkling with candelabras and chandeliers.

Robbie stopped short. He couldn't go up to the door. There was a big party going on! He turned to go—then hesitated. He couldn't go home, either. Papa was sick—maybe even dying. He *had* to get help.

Pushing down his misgivings, Robbie quickly slipped through the wide-open gate, skirted the carriages on the driveway, and headed for the back door. He could hear music and laughter inside the house. Climbing the steps up to the kitchen door, he knocked. He had to knock loudly several times before the door finally opened. At the last minute Robbie pulled his cap off his head.

A young maid—maybe Peter's age—looked at him quizzically. "What do you want?" she asked.

"P-please, miss, I need t-to speak to Miss Nightingale—Miss Florence," Robbie stammered.

"Huh! I don' think you'll do any such thing tonight," the girl said. "There's fancy goings-on."

"I know, but—"

"Why's that door open?" hollered a sharp voice from inside the kitchen. A huge form wearing a lopsided, puffy, white cook's hat appeared beside the girl.

"Someone to see Miss Florence," the girl smirked.

"What? Go away, boy. Miss Florence don' have time for the likes of you tonight. Shoo, shoo! Go on, now!" The door swung shut, but not before Robbie heard the cook mutter, "Miss Flo do a good turn for the riff-raff 'round here, and the next thing you know they're walking right up knocking on the door." *Slam*.

Robbie jammed his cap back on his head. Now what was he supposed to do? He made his way back along the side of the large house. As he came abreast of the veranda, he saw another carriage pull up to the wide steps and a handsome couple get out. The front door of the big house was wide open in the warm June evening. A butler took the man's hat and walking stick, while a lovely young woman in a green silk gown greeted her guests.

"Oh, Flo, you look divine tonight!" giggled the lady guest before she swept inside.

Robbie's eyes widened. Miss Florence herself was on the veranda—this was his chance!

Without thinking of the consequences, Robbie dashed around the bushes and up the smooth, stone steps. "Miss Florence!" he panted, tugging on her skirt. "Please come quickly—it's my father! He's sick and—"

The butler turned, thunder in his eyes. "You, boy! Go away before I throw you down the steps!" The butler's hand grabbed Robbie by the collar.

"No, wait—it's all right," said the young woman's

13

calm voice. Miss Nightingale bent slightly and peered into Robbie's face. He caught a whiff of rose perfume. "You are—?" she asked.

"Robbie Robinson, miss," he gulped, remembering to snatch the cap off his head once more. "It's Papa—he's bad sick, and Mama sent me to fetch you. That is, if you'll come."

Florence Nightingale straightened. "Of course I'll come. I know your family. Your mother wouldn't have sent for me if I wasn't needed. Wait here one moment, Robbie." The young woman disappeared through the front door, leaving Robbie alone with the glowering butler. In a moment, she was back.

"Where do you think you're going, Florence?" a shrill voice followed her from the front door. Robbie saw an elegant woman in a cream-colored gown clutching her throat anxiously.

"It's all right, Mother," said Miss Nightingale quickly. "I'm needed in the village." And she took Robbie's arm and hustled him down the front steps, past the astonished faces of arriving guests.

"You can't leave now, Florence!" her mother called behind them. But the firm hand of Miss Nightingale pushed Robbie down the driveway, past the carriages, and out the front gate.

Robbie was speechless at first. He could hardly believe he was walking down the road with such a fine lady as Miss Nightingale. But she talked easily, asking him what was wrong. Finding his voice, Robbie told her about the trip to London and Papa getting sick with constant vomiting and diarrhea.

When they turned in at the small cottage, the early summer twilight was almost gone. Margo was still on the step, rocking back and forth with a sleeping baby Mae in her arms. She stared at Miss Nightingale's shiny green dress, but all she said was, "Peter's home—putting Sissy and Tommy to bed. He didn't find no work today."

Florence Nightingale went right into the cottage. Robbie was suddenly aware of the stink—the smell of sickness, dirty bedding, and an overfull slop pot. But the lady didn't seem to notice. She talked quietly with Robbie's mother, who was wringing her hands.

"It sounds like cholera," Miss Nightingale said grimly. "Your husband must have picked it up in London—there's an epidemic there. He's dehydrated—we must get some fluids into him if we can."

The two women went into action. Robbie shrank back into the shadows and was soon joined by Peter. Silently the two brothers watched as Miss Nightingale cradled their papa's head in her arms and tried to spoon water down his throat. But as soon as she got some down, he gagged and threw it up.

As the hours dragged on, Robbie's eyes closed and his head nodded. With a start he woke up, trying to remember what was happening. Peter was slumped, asleep on the floor beside him. A single candle flickered near his parents' bed, and he could hear murmuring female voices.

"You have a healing gift, Miss Florence, you do," his mother was saying.

"You can't say that, Mrs. Robinson," said Miss

Nightingale sadly. "Your husband is a very sick man. He—he may not make it."

"I know," said Mrs. Robinson, her voice catching. "But your presence is healing, even in the midst of our suffering. You'd make a fine nurse."

Miss Nightingale gave a bitter laugh. "I wish my mother thought so. She thinks nursing is a 'vile profession'—staffed by lowerclass women who are too rough mannered to be proper housemaids. Or worse, bawdy girls who want to flirt with doctors and sick soldiers."

"My, my, she does think badly," said Mrs. Robinson. "But you're not a girl, Miss Florence. You're a grown woman! You could be a nurse!"

Again the short, bitter laugh. "I'm thirty-two. But you don't know my parents, Mrs. Robinson. In my social class an unmarried daughter is as tied to her parents' wishes as a schoolgirl."

Just then the man on the bed groaned and thrashed about. The horrible retching began, the dry sounds of gagging and coughing with nothing to spit up. Robbie squeezed his eyes shut and put his fingers in his ears. He couldn't stand to hear his father suffer so!

After a while, Robbie realized the retching had stopped. Slowly he lowered his hands and opened his eyes. In the dim candlelight his mother's eyes were wide, stricken.

"I'm sorry, Mrs. Robinson," said the sad, sweet voice of Miss Nightingale. "Your husband's suffering is over...but yours, dear woman, is just beginning."

Chapter 2

Drummer Boy

THEY BURIED THOMAS ROBINSON in the churchyard of Wellow Village. Not many villagers came to the cottage to express their sympathy. They were too afraid of the cholera.

At Florence Nightingale's urging, Thomas's soiled bedding and clothing were burned and buried behind Cinder's shed. Sally Robinson put Peter, Margo, and Robbie to work scrubbing the cottage floor. She boiled all their dishes and cooking pots, their drinking water, and their clothes.

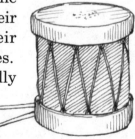

But when it was done, Sally Robinson sat at the table in the cramped cottage and just stared at her hands. "I-I don't know what we're going to do now," she whispered. "How am I ever going to feed the seven of us?"

"I've been thinking, Mama," Peter spoke up. He cleared his throat, manly like. "Papa wasn't having much luck getting jobs lately—even with two of us to load and carry. I think I should take Cinder and the cart to London and sell 'em—get a better price for them in the city. That money should tide you and the younguns over till I get my first wages."

"Your first—what do you mean, wages?" said his mother warily. "You're a good boy, Peter, but I don't recall jobs hanging like gooseberries from bushes. What kind of job be you thinking of?"

Peter cleared his throat again. "I'm gonna join the British army, Mama," he said, his words suddenly spilling out in a rush. "When Papa and I were in London, I talked to a soldier in the Seventeenth Lancers. They're looking for more volunteers. I'm good with horses; I'd have a chance. A soldier gets regular wages, and I could send it home to you."

Sally Robinson stared at her eldest son. "But— the army? I don't want to lose you, too."

"Ah, Mama," Peter scoffed. "England hasn't fought a war for thirty years! It's mostly drill and parades and putting on a show to scare off our enemies."

Robbie's mouth hung open. Peter, a soldier? What an absolutely wild, glorious, wonderful idea. His chest ached with jealousy.

"That's not all, Mama." Peter glanced at Robbie, then took a breath. "Robbie could get a job, too—as a drummer boy." The tall, gangly lad rested his hands on the table and leaned eagerly toward his mother. "Don't you see? *Two* sets of wages coming back to you—regular like! *And* two less mouths to feed."

Sally Robinson's eyes were big, desperately trying to make sense of what Peter was saying. "But—but what about me and Margo and the little ones? What would we do without all our menfolk?"

Margo marched up to the table, hands on her hips. "You're forgettin', Mama. I'm fourteen years old—almost a woman. I can do a woman's work—take in laundry, or maybe get a job as a kitchen maid at one of the big houses. We can get by without the boys." She tilted her chin at her brothers with a smug if-you-can-do-it-I-can-too look.

Robbie was in shock. He had expected his mother to forbid the very idea of his going with Peter to join the army. But Mama and Peter and Margo were talking and worrying and making plans all at once.

The door of the cottage stood open, catching the warm June breezes. Robbie squinted his eyes at the dirt road that led out of Wellow, past the Nightingales' estate, and on toward London.

He imagined himself wearing a plumed hat and red uniform with its white belts crossed over his chest. He imagined the wooden drumsticks in his hands and the *rat-a-tat-tat* as they struck the drum.

Could it actually happen? He, Robbie Robinson, a drummer boy in Her Majesty's Army?

✧ ✧ ✧ ✧

Never in all his life had Robbie Robinson imagined that he would ever leave England, much less end up sleeping in the mud in the Crimea—a wild, unfriendly hunk of land on the underbelly of Russia.

Robbie had never heard of the Crimea before. He'd been drummer boy for the Sixty-Eighth Infantry for almost two years now, but so far it had mostly meant doing parade drills and running errands for the soldiers and polishing their boots. He didn't mind the dirty work so much; most of the soldiers were good-hearted blokes, even if they did boss him around a lot. It was worth it to strut at the head of the Sixty-Eighth in his smart red coat with the white belts crossed over his chest, beating the snappy march beat on his drum.

When young Queen Victoria came to review her troops, Robbie got to see Peter's cavalry regiment, the Seventeenth Lancers, all decked out in royal blue coats, tight pants and boots, and helmets with stiff plumes. Peter rode a long-legged bay horse named Wolfgang, and Robbie thought how proud Papa would be to see how Peter and Wolfgang wheeled and turned and trotted in exact precision with the rest of his regiment. Proud, too, of the soldiers' pay they sent home every month to Mama and Margo and the little ones.

But suddenly, everyone was talking war. Headlines on the *London Times* in early 1854 blared: "Turkey Declares War on Russia! Calls On Allies to Join Them in the Crimea." Robbie couldn't read the newspaper, but a young private named William

Jones—who was maybe sixteen—tried to explain it to him.

"Ya see, Robbie," he had drawled importantly, "there's this narrow river of water that cuts through Turkey from the Black Sea to the Mediterranean Sea. The Strait of Bosporus, I thinks they calls it. The *Times* says the Russians are gathering troops in the Crimea for an assault across the Black Sea. But you can bet a Queen's shilling the English aren't going to let the Russians get their hands on that strait. It's the gateway to the whole Middle East!"

Sure enough, that spring the members of the Sixty-Eighth Infantry found themselves crammed on a naval ship sailing across the Mediterranean. Robbie spent the first few days at sea below decks on his pallet, moaning with seasickness. When he finally got used to the ship's rolling and pitching and made his way up to the top deck, he saw William at the rail, looking rather ashen.

"I see you got tired of the stink below decks, too," said the older boy, managing a weak grin. William jerked his head at the white sails of other ships scattered before and behind the H.M.S. *Andes*. "See those ships? The British navy is ferrying practically the whole British army to the Crimea. And you shoulda seen those Scottish Highlanders in their plaid skirts and broadswords!"

"I saw 'em," Robbie said, feeling a little irritated. William acted like Robbie didn't know anything. "My brother's on one of those ships—he and his horse, Wolfgang. They belong to the Seventeenth Lancers."

"Your brother? Part of the Light Horse Brigade? Good show!" William looked impressed.

Robbie turned his face away and stared at the billowing sails in the distance. Knowing that Peter's regiment was being sent to the Crimea, too, was the only thing that kept him from feeling overwhelmed by homesickness. He was only twelve years old. What was he doing on a troop ship in the middle of the Mediterranean Sea?

The fleet finally turned north along the coast of Turkey. William and Robbie stood at the rail with other soldiers and sailors as the *Andes* lowered its sails, stoked up its auxiliary engine, and steamed through the Strait of Bosporus. They stared as the graceful domes and needlelike minarets of Constantinople, Turkey's capital city, slipped past them on the western shore. On the opposite shore sprawled Scutari, a "suburb" of the capital city separated by the strait.

"Look up there!" William pointed to a large, ugly, fortress-like building perched on a hill beyond the Scutari waterfront. "Wonder what it is?"

"That ugly monster used to be a barracks for Turkish soldiers," one of the sailors snorted. "Been turned into an army hospital, I hear."

I sure hope I never see the inside of that awful place, thought Robbie.

And then the H.M.S. *Andes* steamed into the Black Sea.

✧ ✧ ✧ ✧

Now it was October, and Robbie was already heartily sick of war.

The drummer boy sat brooding on an upturned bucket, trying to clean the mud from his drum and field pack with his one good hand. Everything was going wrong!

He had only seen real action once so far, and that had been a few weeks earlier at the Alma River. In that fight, a piece of shrapnel had injured his left hand. Though the Russians had retreated somewhat, and the battle was counted as an Allied victory, the Russians had nevertheless retained control over Sebastapol, their primary fortress in the Crimea. "Don't know what kind of victory it is when we lost almost two thousand men dead or wounded and didn't even take the place," Robbie muttered to himself, giving a vicious swipe with his rag to the drum.

The wound to his own hand hadn't seemed too serious, but it was still painful and his fingers were stiff, making it difficult to play his drum.

At least Peter was safe, Robbie reminded himself. Lord Raglan, the British field commander, had held the Light Horse Brigade back. Peter and the rest of the Light Brigade had been champing at the bit to join the action. But Lord Raglan was firm. When a pushy *London Times* reporter asked why, Lord Raglan said he needed the Light Brigade to be "the eyes and the ears of the army"—scouting out the terrain and keeping track of where the enemy was.

After the battle at the Alma River in September, Robbie's infantry division had set up camp a few miles south of Sebastapol, using big guns to bombard the Russian fortress. The cavalry, meanwhile, had set up headquarters about five miles farther south at Balaklava, a sleepy Russian village with a small, natural harbor on the Black Sea, where the British ships were riding at anchor.

Now it was late October and they were just waiting—waiting for Sebastapol to fall, or waiting for the great Russian army to ride out of the scrub forests near Balaklava. Meanwhile, the chilly fall rains combined with the churning feet of thousands of cavalry horses, troops, wagons, mounted guns, and pack animals had turned all the camps into swamps of mud.

It was the waiting...and the mud...and the cold...and the gag-awful rations—salt pork and dry biscuit—day after day that was getting to Robbie. Not only that, half the supplies had been left behind to make room to transport the wounded and sick back across the Black Sea to Barracks Hospital in Scutari. So while the French soldiers slept in canvas tents, many of the British troops slept on the muddy ground rolled up in their thin, damp, wool blankets.

No wonder half the army was sick.

Robbie threw down the rag, giving up on his hopeless task. He cradled his injured hand with his good arm, trying to warm his chilled fingers, and glared gloomily at the toes of his boots.

"How's the hand?" said a familiar voice.

"Peter!" he cried, jumping off the bucket—and the next minute landed on his backside *splat!* in the mud. Pain shot from his hand up his left arm.

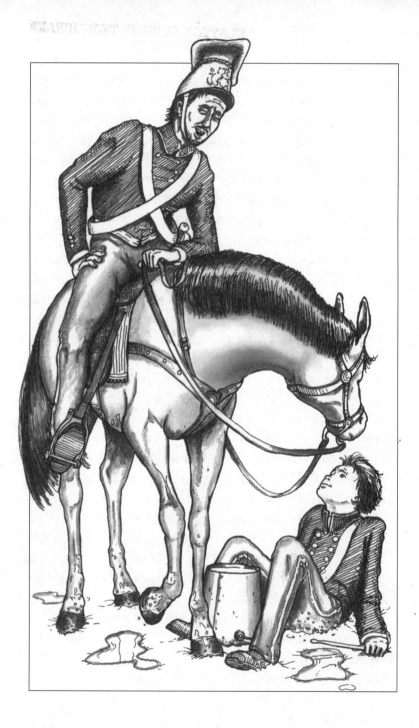

Laughing apologetically, Peter sprang off Wolfgang's back and gave Robbie a hand up

Robbie noticed with a twinge of satisfaction that Peter's boots and Wolfgang's legs and belly were splattered with the same dull brown mud that now covered the seat of his pants.

Peter recovered the bucket and took Robbie's seat, giving his little brother a critical once over. "You're not sick, are you? Is the hand healing all right? Are you getting enough to eat?"

Wolfgang nuzzled Robbie, as if looking for a treat. "My hand's all right, I guess," Robbie shrugged, wishing he had a fat, sweet carrot to give the horse. "No, I'm not sick. But what I wouldn't give for some of Mama's steak and kidney pie."

Peter laughed ruefully. "Yeah. Me too."

Robbie resisted the urge to throw his arms around his big brother. It wouldn't be "soldierly." But he desperately wanted to beg Peter to stay. It was only five miles to Balaklava, but the only time he got to see his brother was when Peter made a point to take a "long cut" through the Sixty-Eighth Infantry camp whenever he was assigned an errand.

"Wolfgang looks thin," Robbie said, scratching the cavalry horse's neck.

Peter winced. "Yeah. The animals are suffering just as much as the men. We took ten more of the Lancers down to the harbor today. Sick with cholera. Some are so far gone, I don't think they'll last the night. But the ship won't sail till they get enough sick—or wounded—to justify the trip." Suddenly

Peter's shoulders sagged, the helmet dropped into the mud, and his head sank into his hands.

Robbie was alarmed. Peter couldn't lose heart—not Peter. Robbie relied on his older brother to keep his chin up, to talk up the glory of the British army and the noble cause they were fighting for!

But Peter's voice became almost a moan, muffled in his hands. "The whole Light Brigade is down to six hundred men, Robbie. Lancers, Dragoons, Hussars—together we've lost over four hundred men already, and almost all of those are dead or dying of sickness and bad food, not battle wounds!"

Robbie knew it was true. Even before the British troops had landed on Russian soil, hundreds of soldiers had died of cholera. Since then, conditions had gone from just unpleasant to downright miserable.

"Robbie! Robbie! Did you hear?" Robbie turned his head and saw William slipping through the mud toward them. His friend's thin face looked excited. "Oh—Peter. I didn't know you were here." The young soldier looked confused. "Were you the messenger?"

"Messenger?" Robbie asked. "For whom?"

Peter plucked his helmet from the mud and stood up. "Yes. I brought a message for Lord Raglan." His voice had changed, back to his confident, matter-of-fact self. "A squad from the Light Brigade discovered thousands of Russian troops massing for an attack on Balaklava." Peter swung up into the saddle.

He gave Robbie a brief salute before wheeling Wolfgang around and calling back over his shoulder, "They could attack by dawn tomorrow!"

Chapter 3

Into the Valley of Death

I NEED AN ASSISTANT," a booming voice was insisting. "Can't you spare even one soldier to—"

"Mr. Russell!" Robbie, rolled up in his blanket and using his pack for a pillow, recognized Lord Raglan's voice, polite but irritated. "The British army is not required to provide newspaper reporters with a staff. That is your business. It is quite enough that we suffer your presence when a battle is afoot. If you must come with me to Balaklava, we need to leave— immediately."

Robbie poked his head out of his blanket. The sky was gray with dawn, but the sun had not yet come

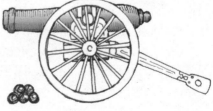

up. William still lay beside him, asleep. Curious at the commotion, Robbie rolled out of his blanket, taking care not to put any weight on his throbbing left hand, and made his way around a stack of supply crates to where the voices were coming from.

Lord Raglan was easy to recognize. The commander of the British army had lost his right arm many years earlier fighting Napoleon, and his limp coat sleeve was tucked in the belt of his uniform. Even so, he sat regally on his muscular chestnut horse.

Mounted on another horse was a big man in civilian riding clothes. He had bushy black eyebrows with a full beard and moustache. *That must be the newspaperman*, thought Robbie, gawking at the assembly of officers from several different regiments.

Just then the newspaperman caught sight of Robbie.

"Wait a minute," he bellowed. "That boy there—who is he?"

Lord Raglan was having trouble being patient. "Well, boy?" he snapped. "State your name and regiment."

"M-me?" Robbie stammered. Then he caught himself and stood stiffly at attention. "Robbie Robinson, sir, drummer boy, Sixty-Eighth Infantry."

"But the boy's hand is injured, Lord Raglan," crowed the reporter. "Surely he can be spared from his duties as drummer boy for one day—if, indeed, he shouldn't already be excused from them until he heals!—during which, he could be immensely useful to *me*."

Lord Raglan, eager to be done with this interruption, dispatched an aide to speak to Robbie's captain. Five minutes later Robbie found himself being hauled up behind the saddle of broad-backed William Russell, correspondent for the *London Times*. As they rode out of the camp, Robbie caught sight of William, hair tousled, mouth hanging open, staring after them with unabashed envy.

Within half an hour, Lord Raglan and his staff had traveled five miles southeast toward Balaklava at a steady walk-trot. Just as the sun rose on the far horizon in front of them, the plateau they were on suddenly dropped away about six hundred feet to the valleys below.

Lord Raglan held up his hand to halt. Unable to see around Mr. Russell's big back, Robbie slid off the horse and stared wide-eyed at the sight below.

About two and a half miles to the south on their right, Robbie could see the tall masts of British troop ships riding at anchor in the small harbor of Balaklava. Stretched out like a V toward the east in front of them were two long valleys, separated by a low ridge. The valley on the right, nearest Balaklava, was simply called the South Valley. The one to the left side of the ridge was the North Valley. Each was about a mile wide and three miles long. At the far ends both valleys ended abruptly in a mass of hills.

Lord Raglan lifted his hand-held telescope and surveyed the scene below. "Look there. The Russians have set up their guns at the far end of the North Valley," he muttered to his aide. "And it looks like they have more cannons on the hills there to the left, overlooking the North Valley. Where are our guns?"

"Along the ridge between the valleys, sir, aimed into the North Valley," said the aide. "Manned by the Turks, I believe."

Robbie squinted into the rising sun. Sure enough, at the far end of the North Valley, he could make out an indistinct mass of gray-coated cavalry, and in front of them what looked like a row of ten or twelve heavy guns. And on the ridge running between the two valleys, he could see knots of Turkish soldiers digging in around small clusters of cannons.

"Sunrise...October 25, 1854...overlooking Balaklava...all is tense and quiet," muttered Mr. Russell's voice. The newspaperman was standing just behind Robbie's shoulder, jotting notes on his pad of paper. Then he asked abruptly, "How many Allied guns do you see on the ridge, Robinson?" Apparently, the newspaperman's eyesight wasn't so good.

Robbie squinted and counted. "Four strongholds dug in along the ridge, sir. There's usually two or three cannons in each stronghold."

"And the British regiments?"

Robbie pointed toward the harbor. "There, just north of the village, holding the line between the South Valley and the harbor. They're the Ninety-Third Scots Highlanders—"

"Looks like a bloomin' fancy-dress ball with those plaid kilts and big bearskin hats," muttered Russell.

"—and just below us," Robbie went on, scanning the foot of the plateau on which they were standing.

"See? Here, at this end of the South Valley. Both the Heavy and Light Brigades are mounted and ready." Then, swelling with sudden pride, he added, "My brother is down there, sir. Private Peter Robinson, Seventeenth Lancers."

"Brother, eh?" Mr. Russell's pencil scribbled. "What are they all doing in the South Valley?" he growled. "They can't see a thing with that ridge between them and the Russians. Don't the fools know they're outnumbered by the enemy about five to one?"

Robbie looked at the newspaperman sharply. But suddenly he jumped as the guns on the ridge boomed, shattering the stillness. Robbie's heart beat fast. The Turks were firing their twelve-pounders, and the Russians were advancing!

Lord Raglan kept his telescope trained on the ridge, occasionally speaking urgently to one of his staff who then sent a messenger riding down into the valley, taking the commander's orders to the officers below.

"What the—?" William Russell swore under his breath. "The Russians are scaling the ridge, trying to take control of the guns—hey! They've got the Turks on the run!"

It was true. Robbie could see hand-to-hand fighting around the strongholds dug along the ridge—and small figures running down the south side of the ridge into the South Valley. They ran past the Scots Highlanders toward the village.

Robbie tried to answer the newspaperman's questions, but it was hard to concentrate. While the battle raged on the ridge, the officers clustered around Lord Raglan buzzed with dismay, all suggesting various strategies at once. Then, suddenly, the Russian cavalry broke through the ranks on the ridge and swept down the other side, straight toward Balaklava! It looked like mass murder, mounted Cossacks against a small company of infantry. But the Ninety-Third Scots Highlanders, on foot and greatly outnumbered, didn't flinch. The front line knelt and fired, even as the second and third lines fired over their heads.

To Robbie's amazement, the thin red line of Scots Highlanders held, and the Russians turned back!

A great cheer rose from the cavalry regiments below. But it was obvious that the Allies needed more infantry support. Lord Raglan barked another order and sent a messenger hightailing it back toward Sebastapol to bring the First and Fourth Infantry divisions.

Well, at least William will get to see some action after all, thought Robbie wryly. He recalled the look on William's face that morning. His friend couldn't stand seeing Robbie go off to the battlefront while he stayed behind.

So far the fighting had been a mile or so away. But now, just below them, Robbie saw the Heavy Horse Brigade get in formation behind their commander, Sir James Scarlett, and head toward the fighting in the South Valley. Not a moment too soon, for suddenly another wave of Russian cavalry swept over the ridge and down to meet them. Even on top of the plateau, Robbie could hear the high-pitched attack yells, the clang of swords and sabers, the screams of wounded men and animals.

It seemed like hours—maybe it was only minutes—but just as suddenly as they had come, the Russians wheeled their chargers, scrambled back over the ridge, and retreated into the North Valley, leaving their dead and wounded.

Robbie looked sharply at Lord Raglan, head to head with his staff officers. What was he going to do now? Were the Russians in retreat? Was the battle over? Once again the commander raised his telescope, scanning the valleys and the ridge between. Even without a telescope, Robbie could see that the Russian cavalry had simply regrouped behind their cannons.

But what was happening up on the ridge? It looked like the Russians were getting ready to haul away the captured Allied guns.

"Captain Nolan!" barked Lord Raglan. "Take this order to Lord Cardigan."

Robbie's heart leaped. Lord Cardigan was the commander of the Light Brigade. *No!* Robbie thought anxiously. *Lord Raglan can't send in the Light Brigade! Why doesn't he hold them back, like he did at the Alma River?*

"Tell Cardigan to follow the enemy and try to prevent them from taking away the guns. They will be supported by the infantry, which I have ordered to advance on two fronts."

Captain Nolan, an excellent horseman from the Eleventh Hussars, kicked his horse into a gallop and rode wildly down the steep slope toward the Light Brigade.

"What infantry?" growled William Russell in Robbie's ear. "Do you see any infantry? They haven't arrived yet."

Robbie's mouth went dry. At the foot of the plateau, he could see Captain Nolan shouting at Lord Cardigan, throwing his arm toward the North Valley, which was not visible to them because of the ridge. Lord Cardigan seemed angry or disbelieving at first. Then, abruptly, he ordered the Light Brigade to fall in and, leaving the South Valley, headed around the end of the ridge until they entered the west end of the North Valley. Robbie saw Captain Nolan fall in with the Hussars behind Lord Cardigan.

"What the—?" muttered Mr. Russell. "Didn't Raglan order them to take back the guns on the ridge? They look like they're lining up for a charge straight up the valley! The fool! What does Cardigan think six hundred Light Brigade can do against three thousand Cossacks?"

Robbie stared. It was true. Just below them, the Light Brigade was lining up behind Lord Cardigan, and the Lancers were in the front line! Robbie thought he could see Peter sitting stiffly on Wolfgang, lance held ready.

"What in blazes?" thundered Lord Raglan, who suddenly realized what was happening. "The man

misunderstood my order! Doesn't Cardigan know the Russians still have control of our guns up on the ridge? It's a three-sided trap! Surely he isn't going to—"

But just then the solitary figure sitting on horseback in front of his troops raised his sword and gave the signal to advance. Behind Lord Cardigan, the Seventeenth Lancers began to advance at a walk, calmly, deliberately. Again Cardigan's sword lifted, and the neat rows of Lancers, Hussars, and Dragoons immediately moved into a trot.

The newspaperman near Robbie swore under his breath. "This is madness," he gasped. "Downright suicide!"

Suddenly, a lone rider pulled out from the Hussars and rode forward at a gallop, cutting in front of the Lancers and riding madly toward Lord Cardigan. "No! No!" a voice screamed. "Not the far guns! The guns on the ridge!"

It was Captain Nolan!

But just then the Russian-held guns on either side of the valley roared and smoked—and suddenly Captain Nolan's chest was drenched in blood. Some of the horses in the ranks stumbled and went down. But the ranks of the Light Brigade just closed in and continued forward at a trot.

Lord Cardigan rode forward rigidly, seemingly oblivious of both Captain Nolan's efforts to redirect him, and the guns booming to the right and left. He raised his sword again—

Instantly, the Light Brigade sprang into a mass gallop, thundering toward the line of guns at the far end of the valley. The mounted Cossacks didn't move, but the line of guns in front of them belched smoke and roared. To Robbie's horror, he saw horses and men of the Light Brigade going down on all sides. The seconds seemed like an eternity, while the Light Brigade kept on charging the full length of the valley. And then, all was confusion as the Light Brigade rode straight between the guns, swords flashing. Even from three miles away, screams and yells filled the air, some human, some from dying horses. Blue and red and gray coats mingled and tangled in a blur at the far end of the valley.

Robbie stood frozen at the top of the plateau, watching the slaughter below him. And then he saw a solitary figure riding back toward them, still in the saddle, coming at a slow walk. It was Lord Cardigan retreating without his men. All around him, riderless horses galloped frantically around the valley floor, crazy with terror.

Suddenly, Robbie moved. Peter! Peter was somewhere down there. He had to find Peter!

He hardly realized how he got down the steep slope of the plateau. Picking himself up at the bottom, he half ran, half stumbled toward the dead and dying strewn all over the North Valley. He had to find Peter...he had to help Peter—

Robbie didn't see the runaway horse coming at him from the side. But he suddenly felt himself flying through the air. As he landed with a thud on the hard, stony valley floor, everything went black.

Chapter 4

Barracks Hospital

ROBBIE FELT HIMSELF being rolled over and fingers pressing against his neck. Then a voice which seemed to be coming from a great distance yelled, "Hey! This one's alive! Bring that cart over here!"

Only semiconscious, Robbie heard shouts...guns booming...moans and cries, but it all seemed far, far away. He was lifted into a cart which was already full of wounded soldiers. Robbie squeezed his eyes shut and tried to think. What happened? Why did his body hurt every time the cart jolted on the rough ground? But the effort was too great. In a few minutes Robbie felt himself sinking back into the peaceful darkness.

✧ ✧ ✧ ✧

Robbie opened his eyes. Above him he saw the tall masts of a ship, swaying with the gentle swells of the tide. But the light was fading; two or three pinpricks of starlight could be seen in the darkening sky.

Then he remembered: *Peter*. He'd been looking for Peter. And suddenly it all came back, like a fist in his stomach.

The Light Brigade had charged the Russian cavalry and their big guns.

Painfully, Robbie tried to sit up. He pushed with his feet and good hand on the deck until his back was against the ship's port gunwale. Wounded men were lying to the right and left of him, all over the deck. Some were lying still and unconscious; others were moaning and calling for help. Still others were half sitting up like Robbie, arms and heads propped up on their knees. Other uniformed men were stepping over the bodies, carrying more wounded and trying to find deck space to put them down.

Gradually, Robbie became aware of voices calling and arguing, but he didn't try to sort it out. Then he thought he heard someone calling his name.

"Robinson! His name's Robbie Robinson—just a kid, maybe twelve years old. Drummer boy for the Sixty-Eighth Infantry."

It *was* his name. Someone was looking for him. The voice was vaguely familiar, but who—?

Suddenly a big, bearded face bent down and looked at Robbie. "Ah! Here you are. My God, I'm

41

glad to see you're alive." The man peered closer. "Seems you got yourself banged up pretty good, though."

Now Robbie remembered. It was the newspaperman, William Russell.

Robbie swallowed and tried to speak. "Peter...my brother...Seventeenth Lancers. Is—is he still alive?"

The man snorted. "I don't know, son. It'd be a miracle if he were. They're still trying to sort out the dead and wounded. But—" His voice softened. "I wouldn't get my hopes up. Brave men, every one, but that charge was a suicide mission—a tragedy."

Robbie raised his good hand and grabbed the man by his coat. "Mr. Russell!" he said hoarsely. "Please...find out if Peter—"

William Russell gently loosened Robbie's fingers from his coat. "All right, son. I'll see what I can do."

❖ ❖ ❖

The ship set sail with the next tide. Robbie slept on and off through the night, huddling as close as he dared to the wounded men beside him, trying to keep the wind from slicing through his uniform jacket. As the sky lightened, he heard grunts and shuffling, as if men were lifting something heavy. "Heave!" someone said, followed by a splash. More grunts, another "Heave!" and another splash.

Robbie blinked, then stared. The sailors were throwing bodies overboard. Men who had died during the night.

A sudden thought shocked Robbie wide awake. What if—what if one of those dead men was Peter? What if Peter was one of the wounded on this ship, and Robbie didn't know it? What if he died without Robbie finding him?

Grabbing one of the rigging ropes with his good hand, Robbie hauled himself to his feet. There was something familiar about this ship. He looked about and realized it was the *Andes*, the same ship that had brought the Sixty-Eighth Infantry to the Crimea. He clung to the rope unsteadily, every bone and muscle stiff and aching, but nothing seemed to be broken. The bandage around his left hand was filthy and caked with blood, but that wasn't a new wound.

Encouraged, Robbie let go of the rigging and started to step over the wounded man next to him, but the ship's sudden pitch on the next wave sent him sprawling. Immediately there were curses and groans as he fell across several of the wounded men crowded together on the deck.

"Hey, boy, don't try that till you've got something in your belly!" called a friendly voice. A sailor grabbed Robbie and leaned him back against the ship's side. Then he dipped into the basket he was carrying and held out a shapeless biscuit. "Here, gnaw on this. Not exactly Christmas pudding, but it'll give you strength."

The sailor moved on, handing out the hard pieces of bread to any of the wounded able to eat. He was followed by another sailor with a bucket of water and a dipper. Robbie grabbed the dipper and drank thirstily. Only then did he realize he'd had nothing to eat or drink since the morning before.

After swallowing the last of the dry, salty biscuit, Robbie once more hauled himself to his feet and made his way slowly about the deck, peering closely at the bloodied, dirty faces of the men. There were uniforms from all different regiments—both cavalry and infantry. "Peter?" he kept saying. "Peter Robinson...anyone know if Peter Robinson is here?"

A big, burly sailor brushed past him carrying a long coil of rope. Robbie caught hold of his sleeve. "Mister, did you—did you help bury those men at sea this morning?"

The man glanced at him. "I did. What of it?"

Robbie swallowed, not wanting to ask his question. "Was one of the dead named Robinson? Peter Robinson, Seventeenth Lancers?"

The man's face relaxed ever so slightly. "Can't say for sure, but"—he scratched his stubbly face— "don't think so. Captain has a list, though. You can check it."

Robbie felt a spark of hope. He continued picking his way over the mass of arms and legs, rounded the bow of the ship, and started back the other side, trying to ignore the shredded uniforms and bloody flesh—looking only at faces.

It was fully daylight now, but the sky was gray and overcast. The Black Sea rose and fell with angry waves, and the sails above him snapped and filled tightly with a gusty southwestern wind. Robbie had to cling one-handed to any support he could find as he pushed himself along, trying to ignore the painful throbbing in his left hand and arm.

He had just threaded his way past one of the ship's guns when he heard a garbled voice speak his name. "Robbie...help me!" Startled, Robbie looked this way and that, trying to hear where the voice came from. Then again he heard the rasping whisper, "Robbie, help me!"

Eyes wide, Robbie stared at the slight, boyish form almost at his feet. "William!" he cried. He dropped to his knees and grasped the hand that the older boy was holding out to him. He hardly recognized his friend. William's hair was matted with dirt and blood, his uniform torn and dirty. But it was William's right leg that shocked him the most. The pant leg was almost torn off, and the leg beneath was a pulpy mass of blood and bone and flesh.

Robbie stared in horror—then in a moment recovered and struggled to his feet. "A doctor! This soldier needs a doctor!" he shouted. He lurched over to one of the sailors who had just come up on deck through one of the hatches. "Mister, where's the doctor? My friend needs a doctor *now!*"

"Easy, lad, easy," said the sailor. "We only got one doctor on board this ship—and he's below operating on the worst cases right now."

"Worst cases...below?" Robbie stared at the man. "You mean there are more wounded below deck?"

The sailor snorted ruefully. "Son, there's more than five hundred wounded and sick on this ship—but at the rate they're dying, there won't be that

many when we reach Scutari. Sorry, boy—all we can
do is give this bunch up here enough water and food

to keep 'em alive until we can get 'em to the hospital—and hope they don't catch cholera on top of their saber slashes and bullet wounds."

As the sailor swung himself up a ladder to the forecastle, Robbie sank down beside William. William's eyes were huge and pleading.

"Hang on, William," Robbie said, trying to force comfort into his words. "We'll get you to a hospital."

✧ ✧ ✧ ✧

The trip to Scutari across the Black Sea took ten days. The H.M.S. *Andes* fought bad weather and rough seas, tacking back and forth, first to the east, then to the west, in an effort to reach the mouth of the Strait of Bosporus.

Robbie stayed near William, who seemed to move in and out of delirium. He begged extra water from a sailor and tried to wash the dirt from William's leg. Then he struggled out of his jacket, stripped off his shirt, and used it to wrap around the shattered leg.

Robbie felt weaker each day. But each day he struggled to his feet and picked his way among the wounded, looking for Peter. The sailors wouldn't let him go below—but once, when a hatch was left open, Robbie crept down the ladder and continued his search. Some men without wounds lay moaning and retching. Robbie recognized the signs of cholera and hurried past. Toward the stern of the ship he saw sailors holding down a screaming soldier—and realized with horror that the doctor was cutting off his leg. The boy staggered back toward the hatch, fighting back the sick feeling in his stomach.

Every few hours, day and night, the dead were heaved overboard.

At last the *Andes* dropped anchor in Scutari harbor. All day long the sick and wounded were lowered into longboats and rowed to shore. The lower deck—the so-called "worst" cases—were taken off first. Then the upper deck. Finally, the sailors lifted William, who was all but unconscious, into a sling and lowered him into a boat. A sailor grabbed Robbie and lowered him by the armpits to waiting arms below. He had to clench his teeth to keep from screaming from the pain in his hand and arm.

On shore, the wounded were loaded into Turkish *arabas*—rough, two-wheeled carts—and small, scrubby horses pulled their loads up a muddy, rutted hill to Barracks Hospital. Those who could walk helped each other struggle up the hill.

William was laid in an *araba*. Afraid of getting separated, Robbie grabbed William's boot hanging off the back of the cart and staggered behind. Why was he so weak? Why were his eyes burning?

In a daze, Robbie followed the Turkish carters who were carrying the wounded and sick inside the huge, fortress-like structure. He tried to keep William in sight as flustered medics directed where the flood of casualties from the *Andes* should go. At first William was laid in a large hallway. Robbie sank down beside him and lifted William's head into his lap.

Hours went by. No one brought them any food or

water. Finally, two British medics came and picked up William and took him into a large room. Robbie struggled to his feet and followed. William, who was only semiconscious, was laid on a wooden platform which was a few inches off the floor and went around the perimeter of the room.

"Do you know this soldier's name?" asked a medic.

"Please...can we have something to eat and drink?" Robbie whispered.

"His name?" insisted the medic.

"Private William Jones, Sixty-Eighth Infantry," said Robbie dully. "And I'm Robbie Robinson, drummer, Sixty-Eighth Infantry."

The two men disappeared. A while later a big pot of steaming liquid was brought into the room, ladled into cheap tin bowls, and passed around. Robbie tried to pour some of the liquid into William's mouth, then drank some himself. It tasted like cabbage water with bits of soggy vegetables floating in it.

Still, the warm liquid felt good going down. Robbie lay down on the wooden platform beside William and closed his eyes. He could hear scurrying underneath the platforms—rats! And the stink from the overflowing slop bucket in the corner and so many unwashed men was so strong that Robbie thought the "soup" he'd eaten was going to come back up.

He fell into a fitful sleep. In his dreams he kept seeing the Light Brigade charging up the North Valley toward the line of big Russian guns...saw the horses go down in a swirl of dust and flying legs...saw the swords and sabers slash the air—

He woke up in the dark, sweating. For a few moments, he couldn't remember where he was. Then he heard the scurrying rodents beneath the platforms, heard the moans of wounded men all around him...and fell back on the platform in despair.

Maybe it would have been better to die on the battlefield than end up in a hellhole like this.

In the hallway outside the room, Robbie saw the light of a lamp bobbing along. Then the lamp was carried into the room, throwing large, eerie shadows on the wall. The lamp person was walking quietly around the room, stooping beside each soldier, softly speaking a few words, then moving on.

Robbie squinted his burning eyes and tried to follow the lamp. There was something strangely familiar about this person. The shape and clothes almost looked like a woman—but that was impossible! Then as the figure came closer, Robbie heard the rustle of a long dress on the stone floor.

He raised himself on his right elbow. The light shone on William and a slender hand touched the young soldier's head. Then the lamp and the woman came to where Robbie lay.

Briefly the light swept across the woman's face. Robbie saw soft, wavy, golden-red hair pulled snugly back from an oval-shaped face and tucked beneath a plain white cap.

That face...he knew that face! Was he dreaming? Or...could it really be—

"Miss Nightingale!" he gasped, trembling all over. "It's you!"

Chapter 5

Message From Balaklava

THE WOMAN LOOKED AT ROBBIE, astonished. "You know my name? Who are you?" She held the lamp closer. "Why—you're just a boy."

"It's me, Miss Nightingale. Robbie Robinson, from Wellow Village. Drummer boy...Sixty-Eighth Infantry."

"Yes," she said softly. "I remember." He felt her cool hand touch his face. "Why, you're burning with fever!"

"Don't bother with me, Miss Nightingale," Robbie said hoarsely. "It's just my hand. But William here needs help bad. If he doesn't get it soon, I'm afraid he's gonna die!"

She was silent a moment—then he heard her murmur, "Oh, dear God, why all this slaughter and waste?" She rose abruptly. "I'll try, Robbie. But there're too many wounded, and too few doctors. We've got nurses, but...never mind, that's not your problem. Try to sleep now. I'll do what I can."

Robbie sank back onto the platform and watched as Miss Nightingale's lamp finished going around the room, then was swallowed up into the dark hallway.

❖ ❖ ❖ ❖

Robbie woke to the sound of female voices.

"Empty the slop bucket?" complained a whiny voice. "But, Miss Nightingale, I thought we were supposed to do *nursing*! I didn't come all the way from England to empty slop buckets like a servant."

"Then you misunderstood your calling," said another woman firmly. Robbie recognized Florence Nightingale's voice. "We are here to do whatever needs to be done to help these sick and wounded men. So far, emptying slop buckets seems to be one of the few things the doctors and medics will let us do—so empty slop buckets we will!"

It took a great effort for Robbie to open his eyes. Why did he feel so weak? But at last he struggled up onto his right elbow and looked around. It was morning—at least daylight brightened the grim, dirty windows. Miss Nightingale and another woman had their sleeves rolled up and were struggling with the slop bucket in the corner.

But Robbie sensed that something was wrong. With sudden alarm, he looked frantically around him. Some of the wounded soldiers were still sprawled on the low wooden platform on either side of him in restless sleep; others were sitting up, cursing and muttering under their breath. And then he realized what it was.

William was gone.

"Miss Nightingale!" he tried to shout, but his voice came out weak and hoarse. "Where have they taken William?"

The tall, slender woman hurried to his side. "Hush, Robbie, don't fret. Your friend has been taken to surgery. He is there now. But..." She turned and looked at the young nurse who was standing by the slop bucket, hands on hips, glaring at Miss Nightingale. "Wait a few minutes, Robbie. I'll be right back."

The two women grabbed the handle of the bucket and carefully lugged the stinking container out of the room. In about five minutes, Florence Nightingale was back at his side. Her sleeves had been rolled down, her white cuffs rebuttoned, and her hands smelled like soap. She was also carrying a large pair of scissors.

"Robbie, let me see your left hand," she said. "I need to cut off that old bandage."

Gently she began snipping at the ragged, dirty cloth which had been wrapped around his hand for weeks. "When did this happen?"

"Just a bit of shrapnel...caught me," he said with effort, wincing as the cloth encrusted with dirt and blood pulled at his skin and the sensitive wound. "When we fought the Russians at the Alma River... near Sebastapol."

She looked into his face, eyes flashing. "But that was in September, nearly six weeks ago! And you are just now being sent to the hospital?"

"Ah, no," he muttered, wincing again. "I didn't come because of my hand. I...we...I mean, I was trying to find Peter after the Light Brigade—" He stopped, unable to go on. After a long silence, during which Florence Nightingale kept snipping with her scissors and giving him a sidelong glance now and then, he finally took a breath and said, "Something hit me and knocked me senseless. I thought I'd been shot, but I don't seem to have any more holes in me. But the horses were running crazy...they'd lost their riders. I think one of them—" Again he stopped.

"Where's your brother Peter?" Miss Nightingale asked gently.

Robbie looked at her with feverish, hollow eyes. "I don't know," he whispered. "He wasn't on the *Andes*— the ship that brought William and me here."

She nodded grimly. "There are two more ships in the harbor with wounded from the Battle of Balaklava. And hundreds who are not wounded, but sick—all crammed together, infecting even the mildly wounded." She looked at Robbie's face, gone pale even with the fever bright in his eyes. "I'm sorry, Robbie. I just feel so helpless and angry at all the suffering I see here—some of which could be prevented. I will check the names of the men on the other two ships to see if your brother has been brought here."

With the last snip of her scissors, she tried to remove the bandage from his hand, but it was stuck fast to his wound. Patiently, bit by bit, she finally removed the last piece of dirty rag.

Robbie stared in horror. The wound on the back of his hand was far worse than he had imagined. Pus and blood oozed from the raw wound, and the skin around it was an angry, puffy red.

"No wonder you are ill with fever," said Florence Nightingale. "The shrapnel is still embedded and your hand is terribly infected. Here—we must get your coat off." She helped Robbie struggle out of his dirty uniform jacket; only then did he remember that he had just his long underwear on beneath after using his shirt to bandage William's leg.

Carefully she examined his hand and his arm. Finally she said, "Robbie, look at me." He tried to focus on her face—so kind and gentle. "Your hand is very bad. The infection has started to go up your arm—see these red streaks? The infection is making you sick. *Now listen to me.*" Her eyes locked on to his. "I don't know if your hand can be saved. The important thing is to save your life. Do you understand?"

Robbie tried to focus on Miss Nightingale's face, but the room seemed to be spinning. His whole body was trembling with cold, yet his face and eyes felt burning hot.

From somewhere far away he heard Miss Nightingale's voice, urgent, but tender. "I'm saying,

Robbie, the doctor might have to cut off your hand. You've got to be brave. *It's the only way.*"

✧ ✧ ✧ ✧

Robbie stared at the bandaged stump at the end of his left arm, which hung in a sling. Seven days had passed since they'd cut off his hand. The fever and chills were gone, but he still felt weak and listless. He just sat on the wooden platform in a shapeless, too-large hospital shirt, staring.

He'd been delirious with fever by the time the doctors got around to him. He was half aware of Florence Nightingale checking on him every few hours throughout the night, giving him sips of water, pressing her cool hand to his forehead. And then the medics had come and helped him down a long corridor to the surgery. He stumbled along, supported on either side. Then they'd lifted him onto a table. He tried to ask what was happening, but no one talked to him. A man in a blood-spattered shirt and suspenders barked an order to "hold the boy down!" and he felt heavy hands holding his legs and shoulders and arms.

"Please, Dr. Hall! Give the boy some chloroform," pleaded a woman's familiar voice. Robbie twisted, trying to see Miss Nightingale through the forest of big arms holding him down.

"Nonsense!" snorted the man in the white coat. "These are soldiers. The smart shock of the knife is a powerful stimulant."

56

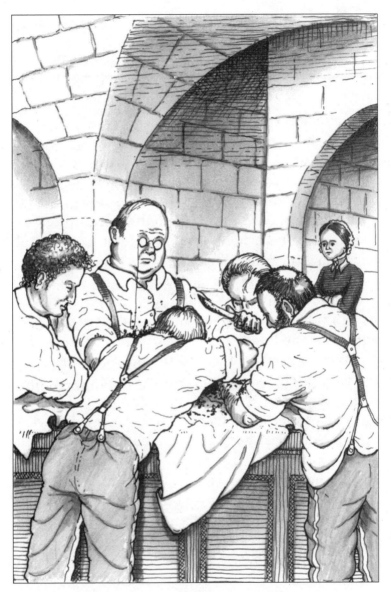

"Soldier?! This is just a boy!" she argued.
"Get out of here, Miss Nightingale," the doctor

snapped, "or I'll have you thrown out! A military hospital is no place for a woman."

Robbie wanted to cry out, *No! Don't go!* But just then he felt a terrible, hot, searing pain in his left wrist. He heard a scream, hardly realizing it was his own scream.

And then he'd fainted.

"Hey," said William, poking him with mock gruffness. "A lot you have to mope about. At least you can get up and walk around. Me—I've lost a leg."

Robbie looked at his friend, half sitting up against the wall. It was true. William's leg had been cut off just below the knee. But, like Miss Nightingale had said, it had probably saved his life.

"I know," muttered Robbie, ashamed. "It's just... what am I supposed to do now? I can't play the drum with only one hand."

"What are *you* supposed to do?" William's voice raised a pitch, sarcastic. He flung a hand out, indicating the other soldiers all around them. "What are any of us supposed to do now? A few will get patched up and sent back to their regiments—maybe to get cut up or shot at again in the next battle. But most of us will hobble home with body parts missing. And the lucky ones—like you—at least have a *home.*"

Robbie frowned at William. "What do you mean? Don't you have a home to go to?"

William laughed bitterly. "Not me. Why do you think I joined the army at sixteen when most blokes my age are still in school—or at least have a job as an apprentice with their father or maybe an uncle."

Robbie shrugged. "Peter was sixteen when he joined the Lancers. Our papa died, and he figured it was a good way to make money to help support Mama."

"Yeah, well, that's good," sighed William. "It's just...I don't have a papa *or* a mama. Never did—at least not that I remember. The army's the closest thing to a family I've got, but they're not going to keep a one-legged private around."

Robbie sat thinking. William was right; it was a lot worse to lose a leg than your hand. Although, he considered glumly, William at least had two hands to do things with, like carve wood or milk cows or hammer a nail—things Robbie would never be able to do again.

The boy shook his head, trying to shake off his gloomy thoughts like a dog shakes off water. He had to stop this! He was going to drive himself mad if he didn't stop feeling sorry for himself.

"Hey," he said to William, "just because you only got one leg doesn't mean you can't get around." He slid off the platform and stood up, feeling slightly unsteady. "I'm going to find you some crutches."

Someone—Miss Nightingale?—had washed his uniform jacket and laid it over him while he slept. Now Robbie put it on, letting his left sleeve hang loose, and carefully made his way to the door. The large hallway was once again filled with wounded soldiers. He stepped over legs and boots, trying not to breathe the now-familiar—but no less unpleasant—smell of sick men, festering wounds, and unwashed bodies. Where had all these men come from?

Surely not still from the Battle of Balaklava!

At the end of the hallway he paused, uncertain which way to go. A medic was stooping over some of the wounded, trying to get names. "Mister," Robbie called out, "where can I find Miss Nightingale?"

"Miss who?" the medic said without looking up. "Oh—the women." He jerked a thumb to Robbie's left, down another long hall.

Robbie kept going, appalled at the number of sick and injured lying everywhere. At this rate, there soon wouldn't be anything left of the British army.

He had to ask twice more before he was directed to a set of small rooms tucked away in a corner of Barracks Hospital. Peeking in at the first door, he saw a large group of women—maybe thirty or forty— all crowded together in a small room, some sitting on chairs, others on the floor. They were all dressed in the same drab, gray tweed dresses with plain white caps on their heads, and a scarf tied loosely around their shoulders. Some of them were ripping material into strips and rolling them into small balls; others were sewing two long pieces of material together.

No one seemed to notice him, so he spoke up tentatively, "Miss Nightingale, please?"

"What's this?" said a pleasant-faced, middle-aged woman nearest the door. "Aren't you a wee thing to be in this place! And—oh, my, he's lost his hand, poor thing." She clucked like a mother hen and drew him into the room. "My name is Mrs. Roberts, laddie. Can we help you?"

Robbie stood there confused. These must be the

nurses Miss Nightingale had mentioned—women who could help sick people! But why were they all sitting here like a sewing party when there were hundreds of sick and wounded men in the hallways?

The hands stopped working, and all the eyes stared at him. To Robbie's horror, he realized he had spoken his thoughts aloud.

"Well, now, I don't blame ye for wondering," said Mrs. Roberts tolerantly. "We've asked Miss Nightingale that ourselves." There was murmuring and nodding around the room. "But military hospitals aren't used to the idea of nurses being good for anything more than scrubbing floors and washing the bed linens—if there were any to wash, God help us." The woman sighed and shook her head. "So right now we're doing what we can to help behind the scenes—like making bandages and sheets to put on the beds."

Robbie had already stuck his neck out, so he said angrily, "But—just do it! Who cares what the stupid doctors think! People are dying out there!" His lip quivered. "Maybe even my brother is out there waiting for someone to help him!"

"Nay, Robbie, we can't just barge in and take over," said a sober voice behind him. He felt Miss Nightingale's hand on his shoulder as she came into the room. "It takes time for doctors to get used to nurses who are trained to ease suffering—especially military doctors, who live in a man's world. If we are to change their ways, we must be patient."

Some of the younger nurses rolled their eyes in disgust, but quickly returned to their tasks.

"Now, Robbie, I'm glad you've come," said Miss Nightingale. "I have a message for you." She handed him a folded paper with a wax seal. "It came by ship with the wounded from the Battle of Inkerman."

Inkerman? There had been another battle? Robbie looked down at the paper. A message for him? His heart beat faster. Maybe—

He looked up into Florence Nightingale's face. "I can't read," he confessed, handing it back to her. "Would you read it to me?"

With a gentle nod she broke the seal, unfolded the paper, and began to read.

To Robbie Robinson, drummer boy, Sixty-Eighth Infantry—sincere greetings.

That same day I left you on board the Andes, *I located your brother, Peter Robinson, Seventeenth Lancers. I regret to say that he died in the charge of the Light Brigade, along with his faithful steed, Wolfgang. I personally helped to bury your brother. He died a hero, Robbie, a courageous soldier who obeyed orders— though I know that fact doesn't ease your terrible loss. He died rebuffing the Russian threat, and you should know that Balaklava remains in British hands, though at a terrible cost in human life.*

I hope this letter finds you recovered from your wounds. Until we meet again, I remain your friend,

William Russell
The London Times

Chapter 6

"I'm Your Man!"

FLORENCE NIGHTINGALE REFOLDED THE PAPER and put it into Robbie's hand. "I'm so sorry, Robbie. I shall write to your mother right away and tell her about Peter's death. She has a right to know."

Robbie stood dry-eyed and stunned. Peter was dead. Died on the battlefield. Died in a suicide charge of six hundred Light Brigade armed with lances, sabers, and swords against Russian guns on three sides and three thousand cavalry.

Just then two medics navigated their way down the crowded hallway carrying a stretcher between them. The man on the stretcher was dead. Robbie barely noticed. But Florence Nightingale rested her arm gently across his shoulders and said quietly, "Dozens of men are dying here each day, after days and weeks of suffering. Peter can't have suffered much if he died where he fell on the battlefield. Maybe...it was a blessing."

For some strange reason, Robbie felt comforted by her words. He knew Peter would rather die that way, as a soldier in the line of duty, out in the open—not as a patient in a stinking, crowded, dark, hellhole of a hospital.

"I need crutches," he said.

Miss Nightingale blinked in surprise at his abrupt request.

"For my friend William," he explained.

"I see." She looked at him thoughtfully. "You're exactly right. We need crutches—lots of crutches—and a whole lot more. More slop buckets, more soap and towels, more mattresses and sheets, more mops and brooms..." Her voice trailed off and she frowned, obviously deep in thought.

Suddenly she turned to Robbie. "Robbie, I need your help. As yet, my nurses and I are not allowed to walk freely throughout the hospital. Even though we were sent here by the Secretary at War, Dr. Menzies, the senior medical officer, and Major Sillery, the military commandant of the hospital, have the last word on what, exactly, we are allowed to do. And *they* aren't inclined to oppose opinionated doctors like Dr. Hall who are absolutely opposed to women nurses."

"But...how can I help *you*?" asked Robbie, confused.

She lowered her voice. "I need you to be my eyes and ears. As one of the patients, no one will question your right to walk about the hospital, getting some exercise. I need to know what supplies the hospital has—and, more importantly, what they don't have but need." She studied Robbie carefully. "In fact, as you begin to feel stronger, I could use a messenger—someone who knows his way about, someone who could go into the town of Scutari—" Florence stopped and smiled apologetically. "But maybe I am asking too much. You are still recovering from surgery and—"

"No!" said Robbie. "It's not too much." He felt a surge of hope, even joy, ease the sorrow that had flooded his spirit at the news of Peter's death. Miss Nightingale needed him. With a wry smile he held up his good right hand. "From now on, Miss Nightingale—I'm your *right-hand* man!"

❖ ❖ ❖ ❖

Robbie took his job as spy seriously. Each day he wandered the hallways of the big army-barracks-turned-hospital, poking his head into the different rooms or "wards," trying to count how many beds were in each, and how many men had to lie on the floor or on the Turkish wooden platforms. He noted that each ward had only one slop bucket, which was used by anywhere from twenty to one hundred men crammed into the room. Men who were too sick to get up just soiled their beds. Most of the men were lying in their dirty long underwear. He also noticed that when a man died, another patient was immediately put into the bed without the sheets or bedding being changed.

Florence Nightingale listened gravely when Robbie reported what he'd found. "No bedpans," she murmured. "It's worse than I feared! We *must* get more supplies! Robbie, did you see a supply room of some kind, where towels or soap or basins or bedding might have been stored and forgotten?"

Robbie shook his head. "No," he said, "but I did see some stairs that go down into the basement. I'll look down there."

"Good!" she beamed. "Be off now—yes, Mrs. Roberts?"

The round-faced, motherly-looking nurse had poked her head into the tiny room that served as Florence's office. "Sister Alice and I are going to market. We'll be back in time for tea. Anything else you want us to get?"

"No, thank you, Mrs. Roberts, I—"

Robbie tugged on her sleeve. "Please, Miss Nightingale, the crutches...for William. I promised him."

She smiled a tired smile. "So you did. Here." She picked up a black cloth purse with long strings and took out a pound note in English money. "Go with Mrs. Roberts and Sister Alice—see if you can find William a pair of crutches."

❖ ❖ ❖ ❖

The crutches were crude, but the way William's

66

eyes lit up, they might have been made of gold.

"Miss Nightingale gave you her own money to buy these for me?" he cried in happy amazement, hopping awkwardly around the room. Each sturdy stick had a padded arm at the top that fit under William's armpit; his hands gripped a small handle lashed to the crutch halfway down.

"I told you she did, didn't I?" Robbie was still flushed with the fresh air and exercise of going to the Scutari market. "But, hoo, boy, that Sister Alice sure talks. Talked my ear off. Did you know that Sister Alice and some of the other nurses are Catholic nuns? And at least one is a Baptist! Miss Nightingale insisted that any woman who feared God and met the qualifications should be accepted as a war nurse, no matter what church they're from."

"But didn't you say they *all* wore ugly gray dresses? I never heard of proper Church of England ladies working with *nuns*—much less dressing alike." William kept thumping back and forth, trying out his crutches.

"That's the point, I guess—to help them work together. Sister Alice says Miss Nightingale has real strict rules, too. If any of the nurses are caught drinking or flirting with any of the soldiers, they get sent straight back to England, third class, on salt rations!"

William laughed. "Hoo, boy. I guess a body don't tangle with Miss Nightingale!"

Robbie lowered his voice and motioned to William to sit down on the wooden platform. "Speaking of women," he half whispered, "I saw something funny when we were coming back from the market. A bunch of women and little kids were going down some narrow steps and into a small side door of the hospital."

"Women and kids!" said William, shocked. "Down? You mean, like, underneath the hospital?"

"Yes!" Robbie's eyes were dancing. "Miss Nightingale wants me to look for any overlooked hospital supplies. We could, you know, look down in the basement...I mean, as soon as you feel like it—and get used to those new legs of yours."

❖ ❖ ❖ ❖

Florence Nightingale's lips parted in shock and for a moment she was speechless.

But Mrs. Roberts was not. "You boys mean to tell us that there are *English* women and children *living* underneath this hospital?"

"Yes, ma'am," said Robbie sturdily, while William nodded vigorously in support. "French and Turkish ladies, too. Soldiers' wives, come to be near their husbands."

"Wives of wounded men?" Mrs. Roberts probed.

Robbie shrugged. "Some, I guess—not all. The army doesn't know what to do with them, so they stuck them in the hospital basement."

"It's pretty dark and dank down there," offered William. "Lots of squalling kids...smoky cooking fires."

"This is outrageous!" exploded Mrs. Roberts, wringing her plump hands. "Why, it can't be healthy, and—what do they do all day? Put a bunch of bored, cranky people together for too long and—"

She was interrupted by a short, amused laugh from Florence Nightingale. "Dear Mrs. Roberts, of course it's outrageous! Everything about war is outrageous. And you are exactly right about those bored women. Back home, I thought there was nothing worse than bored, rich women like myself, busy, busy, busy with endless parties and the latest fashions and gossiping over their needlework. Busy idleness, that's what it was. It nearly drove me mad!"

Robbie stared at Miss Nightingale. He had never seen her like this. Usually she was a model of calmness, her speech firm yet polite and respectful. But now her eyes were flashing fire, and she paced back and forth.

"But these women—away from their own homes, in a strange country, with nothing to do but nurse their babies and wait. It's a disaster in the making." She stopped pacing, her face flushed. "These women need something useful to do—and I know just the thing."

"What?" gasped Mrs. Roberts, astonished.

"The hospital laundry!" Miss Nightingale said triumphantly. "Mrs. Roberts, count how many sheets our nurses have already sewn together. William, will you find Major Sillery, the military commandant of the hospital, and tell him I need to speak to him? And Robbie..." Her gray eyes looked into his own brown ones. "Could you take this letter down to the docks and give it to the captain of the first ship leaving for England? It's very important."

Robbie looked down at the letter. It was addressed to Sidney Herbert, Secretary at War, Houses of Parliament, London.

✧ ✧ ✧ ✧

"Miss Nightingale!" thundered an irritated man's voice. "What is the meaning of this? I go away for three days on military business, and when I return, what do I find? Your nurses have invaded the privacy of the men's wards, unauthorized civilians are doing military laundry, and supplies have been ordered without my permission! This is completely irregular. Explain yourself, Miss Nightingale!"

Robbie stiffened outside the door to Miss Nightingale's room. He had come to tell her that a Turkish cart driver was at the front door of the hospital, his *araba* piled high with scrub brushes, slop buckets, and bedpans. But someone was already with her.

"Major Sillery," said Miss Nightingale, her voice once more measured, calm. "I did my best to locate you to request permission to launder the bedding, but—as you have just said—you were gone, and I could not find anyone who admitted to having authority in your absence. So I simply asked Dr. Menzies if it would be beneficial to put the men into clean beds and clean bedclothes, and he said yes—"

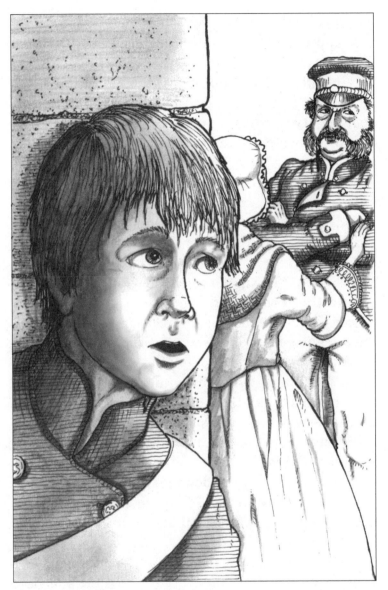

"That," growled Major Sillery, "does not consti-
tute an order."

Miss Nightingale's voice went on, ignoring the interruption. "The 'unauthorized, civilian personnel' you referred to happen to be soldiers' wives, living in this hospital, fed on army rations—in short, the army has, by housing and feeding them, taken responsibility for them."

"Well...we can't let them starve," the commandant muttered.

"Of course not," she agreed smoothly. "But by enlisting their help in laundering the mountains of soiled bed linens, they are earning their room and board, aren't they? As for the supplies that I ordered—"

"Exactly!" The major's voice rose again. "Six thousand cotton bedshirts?! We have a hospital supply officer who is responsible for ordering and distributing supplies. How dare you usurp his authority!"

"I did contact the supply officer about the need," Miss Nightingale went on calmly, "and he shrugged and said none had been ordered by hospital staff so there weren't any to distribute. But since—as you rightly point out—I had no authority to order army supplies, I paid for them myself, and gave them as gifts to our noble, wounded men."

There was no reply. Robbie peeked around the doorway and saw Major Sillery turning red around his stiff, military collar.

Florence Nightingale laid a hand on the major's arm. "Major Sillery, my nurses and I are not here to interfere with your job but to help ease the suffering of our soldiers as best we can. Come—let me show you something."

Robbie ducked away from the door as Miss Nightingale led the major down the hallway and into one of the first wards. The boy, still needing to deliver his message, followed after them.

Several of Miss Nightingale's nurses had just finished gathering dirty bedclothes off the beds and were making them up with the clean, patched sheets the women had sewn together. Most of the men had been stripped of their filthy long underwear, bathed with warm water and soap, and dressed in the clean bedshirts.

One of the soldiers near the door with a head wound grabbed her skirt and said, "God bless ye, Miss Nightingale. These gentle ladies have done us a world of good with their clean sheets and bedclothes. Why, I thought I'd be goin' to my Maker in them dirty long johns! God bless you, too, major," the soldier chortled, saluting. "Best idea you ever had, bringing nurses to this miserable hospital. I hope they gives ye a promotion!"

Major Sillery nodded curtly, turned on his heel, and stalked out of the ward. Robbie had to jump out of the way to keep from being knocked over as the major strode fuming down the hallway.

Chapter 7

Battling the British Army

NOTHING MORE WAS SAID about the hospital laundry by Major Sillery or any of the other medical officers. They just seemed to ignore Miss Nightingale's crew of army-wife volunteers—but at least they didn't hinder them, either.

"Don't you mind, Miss Nightingale," Robbie said stoutly. He was accompanying her on her nightly rounds, holding the Turkish lamp with its paper  chimney to light her way as she quietly visited each of the wards. "British officers don't like being outdone by a woman." He grinned at her. "But the men in the wards—they appreciate what you're doing."

Florence Nightingale chuckled wryly.

"I'm not trying to make the army look bad, Robbie—I'm trying to make them look good! But never mind. It's the sick and wounded who count. As long as we can do something for them..." Her voice trailed off.

It was early December and the rooms felt damp and chilly. "A blanket, miss?" a weak voice pleaded beyond the dim glow of the lamp. "I'm very cold."

"We have no more blankets, soldier," Miss Nightingale said regretfully. "But here—" She slid the knitted shawl off her shoulders. "Wrap yourself in my shawl until we can find some other covering."

Robbie waited until they were back out in the hall before he blurted, "You can't give away your shawl, Miss Nightingale! How will you keep warm? What will the men do if you get sick?"

"If I am cold, it will help remind me to get more blankets, now, won't it?" she said curtly. As they reached the door of the next ward, she turned abruptly to Robbie. "Did you see that man's mouth?"

Robbie frowned, trying to remember. He hadn't been paying much attention. "Well...his gums did seem kind of puffy and bloody."

"Exactly! It's scurvy. If we don't get more fruits and vegetables into these men, we'll have more deaths—deaths that could be prevented!"

They finished their rounds about midnight. "Can you make it back to your room without the lamp?" Miss Nightingale asked Robbie. Her smile was tired. "You're still recovering and should be in bed."

"Don't worry about me," he said gruffly, trying not to sound as exhausted as he felt. "But—what are you going to do?" he asked suspiciously.

"Letters," she said, tilting her chin. "The good Lord encouraged us to 'pray without ceasing'—and I figure it doesn't hurt to ask the powers-that-be in England for what we need without ceasing as well!"

❖ ❖ ❖

One of Robbie's main duties became taking Florence Nightingale's letters to a ship captain or first mate leaving for England. Most of them were addressed to Sidney Herbert, the Secretary at War, though each week there was also a letter for her parents and her older sister, Parthenope.

Robbie liked getting out and about, even though December in Scutari, Turkey, was gray, wet, and miserable. He kept his eyes open for any supplies being unloaded which might help Miss Nightingale.

He had noticed that whenever the businesslike nurse asked Major Sillery about supplies, the major said, "Talk to the supply officer." But whenever she talked to the supply officer, he muttered grumpily that these things took time. Robbie knew Miss Nightingale was frustrated by what she called "poor communication"—but he suspected that Miss Nightingale was being kept in the dark.

What his friend needed, Robbie figured, was her own source of information.

Hunching his shoulders against the biting sea breeze blowing off the Bosporus Strait, Robbie watched a crew of English sailors roll barrel after

barrel down the gangplank of a cargo ship.

"What are we supposed to do with this stuff?" one burly seaman yelled up at an officer on the deck.

"I don't know!" the officer yelled back. "Our orders are to drop it off at Scutari. Just leave it on the dock until that bulldog of a supply officer—" The ship's officer broke off as the man in question came scurrying down the wet, slippery dock. The military supply officer for Scutari was a short, dumpy man, with dark stubble on his face that never grew into a beard but never looked shaved either, and flabby jowls which *did* make him look like a bulldog.

"What are you doing?" the supply officer protested. "What is this stuff?"

"Lime juice!" the officer yelled down from the deck. "It's all yours."

"Lime juice?" The supply officer scowled and quickly rifled through the crumpled papers he was carrying. "What cockamamie nonsense is this? There's no lime juice on the hospital menu. Take it back! We don't want it. There's been some mistake."

"Ha, ha!" laughed the ship's officer, leaning over the bulwark. "Then it's your problem—all twenty thousand pounds of it!"

The supply officer's jowls wobbled and dropped. "Twenty thou—!" He looked like he was choking. "No, no—take it away."

Robbie watched with mild interest as the supply officer and the ship's officer argued back and forth. Maybe he should report this to Miss Nightingale—but he was afraid it was just one more instance of a military mixup. Wasn't it just like the army to send twenty thousand pounds of lime juice, when what the hospital really needed was blankets, or disinfectant, or—or fruit and vegetables, like Miss Nightingale was saying, to help stop that scurvy disease. But it *was* a problem. Where was the army going to get fruit and vegetables in the middle of winter?

Just then Robbie's attention was distracted by longboats coming in to shore from another ship riding at anchor in the harbor. As the oars rose and dipped in the slate gray swells of the harbor, bringing the longboats closer, Robbie could see they were loaded with sick and wounded soldiers.

So many more! he thought. And where were they going to put them? Barracks Hospital was already full to overflowing. In spite of the sick feeling in his gut, Robbie edged closer as the boats were pulled up on the muddy shore, and the bedraggled, groaning men were lifted out and loaded into waiting Turkish *arabas.* One of the two-wheeled carts was stuck in the mud, so as the driver snapped his whip at the straining mule, Robbie stepped forward and helped push with his shoulder against the rickety sides.

The wheels finally lurched out of the muddy rut with a sucking sound—but to Robbie's surprise, the *araba* did not head up the hill toward Barracks Hospital, but turned toward town.

"Where are you going?" he cried in English, running alongside. "The hospital is up there!" He pointed up the hill toward the ugly fortress-like building.

The driver shook his head, rattled off something in Turkish, and drove on. Robbie ran back to another cart, frantically pointing to the hospital on the hill, but all the carts followed the road into town.

"It's all right, boy!" yelled one of the sailors. "Barracks Hospital is too full—this lot is being taken to Scutari General Hospital, the civilian hospital."

Robbie was troubled. He could only imagine the conditions of Scutari General Hospital—which probably didn't have any nurses at all to care for the needs of patients, and now they were going to be flooded with unexpected military casualties. He had to tell Miss Nightingale right away!

He arrived in Miss Nightingale's sitting room/office panting with the strain of trying to run up the rutted, muddy hill. Between gasps, he delivered his startling news, then was immediately ordered to lie down on her couch and rest while she checked out what was happening to this new lot of patients.

Only after lying down was Robbie aware his left arm was throbbing with pain. The cold winter wind and dampness of the harbor had irritated the tender, newly forming skin of the stump where his hand used to be, and it felt like he was being stabbed with a hundred needles. But gradually the throbbing eased, and Robbie fell into an exhausted sleep.

✧ ✧ ✧ ✧

"Robbie." He felt someone shaking his shoulder. "Wake up. I need you to go with me."

Robbie shook his head to clear his mind and looked up into Miss Nightingale's face. She was wearing a cloak and hood, and holding a lantern.

Without asking any questions, he swung his legs

off the couch in her sitting room, put on the cap and neck muffler she was holding out to him, and followed her down the long corridors. As they pushed open the heavy front door of the hospital, battling a cold wind coming off the harbor, Robbie took the lamp so Miss Nightingale could hold her long skirt up from the muddy path that led down the hill. He didn't have to ask where they were going; he knew.

Miss Nightingale was going to do nighttime rounds—when it was less likely she would run into disapproving doctors or huffy medics—at Scutari General Hospital, too.

The mile-long walk to the local hospital became an evening ritual for Robbie and Miss Nightingale, before doing the nighttime rounds at Barracks Hospital. As far as Florence Nightingale was concerned, her responsibility was to any Allied soldier—whether English, French, or Turkish, whether housed at the official military hospital or the local civilian hospital. She immediately began making note of the pressing needs at Scutari General Hospital in the military wards: more slop buckets, bedpans, clean bedding, clean nightshirts, disinfectant, more bandages, warm blankets—the list went on and on.

One evening after slogging the mile through the narrow streets of Scutari, ducking their heads against the sting of sleety snow, Robbie pulled at the door of General Hospital—it didn't budge. Puzzled, Miss Nightingale pulled on the door handle. Still it wouldn't open. Then her lips pressed into a thin line.

"It seems we have enemies here, as well, Robbie,

my man," she said finally. "But if they think they have stopped Florence Nightingale, they are badly mistaken." She looked about for a place to sit, discovering a bench between some dead-looking bushes. "You will just have to return to Barracks Hospital and get a key for me, Robbie. Otherwise, I will sit outside on this bench, probably catch pneumonia, and then Major Sillery will have to answer to The Honorable Sidney Herbert, Secretary at War, for my untimely demise." An almost-smile creased the corners of her determined mouth.

Robbie turned back toward Barracks Hospital, shaking his head. He knew Florence Nightingale was a stubborn woman, but couldn't she give up on a night like this?

It was nearing midnight when Robbie finally trudged back to Scutari General Hospital with a key to the front door. Major Sillery had totally ignored his request—that is, until he informed the major that Miss Nightingale intended to sit outside the hospital until she got in. Now she grinned a welcome at him in the flickering light of the Turkish lamp behind its paper chimney. Her nose was red, but her eyes had a twinkle as she unlocked the door.

"Ain't you mad, Miss Nightingale?" Robbie asked. He was cold to the bone, and his feet were sore. "I sure am. Mad as a cat with its tail in a trap."

"Nay, Robbie," she said, removing her cloak and shaking the snow off it. "What good would it do to get mad? Besides, when people are insulting, they insult God our Maker before they do me."

Chapter 8

Mother Brickbat

THE COLD AND DAMP from the chilly December temperatures seemed to seep into the stone walls of Barracks Hospital. Both Robbie and William caught colds, like many of the other soldiers trying to recuperate from wounds. Rampant diarrhea, scurvy, and malnutrition still made recovery difficult. Florence Nightingale and her nurses rounded up as many braziers as they could find—small, shallow pans which rested on short legs, for burning coal. "But only until we can get proper warming stoves and stovepipes for each ward," she said grimly. And Robbie knew that another letter would be going to Sidney Herbert in England.

More blankets had finally been ordered by Major Sillery at Florence's insistence, but she didn't trust the supply officer to be speedy about it, so she went into the town and bought two hundred blankets with her own money to help fill the need until the army order came in.

"I want you to haunt the docks every day, Robbie Robinson," Miss Nightingale told him, "and tell me the moment those army blankets are unloaded."

So Robbie was down at the harbor the day the ladies landed.

He was used to seeing British sailors and soldiers, Turkish dock workers and merchants, army horses and pack mules milling about the Scutari harbor. But the sight of not one, not two, but *dozens* of British ladies in all manner of dress being rowed to shore from a British sailing ship made him stop in his tracks.

One boatload of ladies holding lacy parasols were laughing and pointing at all the different sights on shore. A rather large group in another longboat wore black robes and their heads were covered with long black veils—Catholic nuns, Robbie guessed. Another two boats landed with women in everyday coats, also flushed with excitement and adventure as they were helped ashore by the seamen.

Robbie stood and stared as the flock of "canaries," "blackbirds," and "sparrows" (as he suddenly pictured them) gathered on the shore. Then one of the nuns, a big, commanding, middle-aged woman, with a square face framed by a white wimple underneath the black veil, stepped forward and asked no one in particular, "Where is Barracks Hospital, if you please?"

Robbie blinked. Barracks Hospital? These women were coming to Barracks Hospital? Why? Was anyone expecting them? What were *they* going to do? He stood rooted to the spot in astonishment until he suddenly realized that half a dozen helpful sailors and soldiers were pointing up the hill.

With a speed that surprised even himself, Robbie scrambled up the muddy hill, ran through the hospital hallways, and burst into Miss Nightingale's office. "They're coming!" he gasped. "Nuns...and ladies...like a big flock of birds...here."

The room was already full of Miss Nightingale's nurses in their plain, gray dresses, white caps, and white aprons, getting instructions for their afternoon chores. A few of the younger nurses giggled.

"Whatever are you talking about, Robbie?" said Florence Nightingale, frowning slightly. "We are busy here and have no time for games." She turned back to the list in her hand.

"No, wait! You must come quickly," he cried, eyes wide. "They'll be here any minute!" Forgetting his good manners, he grabbed Miss Nightingale's hand and dragged her out into the hallway.

As they turned a corner near the front doorway, there in the entryway stood the big nun, surrounded by a large number of women. Robbie heard Miss Nightingale give a little gasp. Then, recovering, she said in a businesslike tone, "May I help you?"

The nun looked her up and down. "Possibly. I am Mother Bridgeman. And these"—she waved her hand vaguely to either side of her—"are Sisters from my convent in Ireland, a delegation of competent nurses, and several English gentlewomen who have come to volunteer their services to our poor, sick fighting men." Mother Bridgeman glanced over Florence Nightingale's shoulder, as if looking for someone.

"We would like to speak to the person in charge." Her Irish brogue rolled thickly off her tongue.

Robbie, once again gaping at the sight of all these strange women, felt Miss Nightingale stiffen beside him. "My name is Florence Nightingale. *I* am the person in charge of nurses and women volunteers at Barracks Hospital," she said coolly. "And I did not ask for you. I was not informed you were coming. And we have no use for you at this time. Thank you very much for coming—but I am sorry. I am sure the next boat back to England will be happy to accommodate you." She turned on her heel as if to go.

There were gasps of dismay from the women gathered like curious schoolgirls behind Mother Bridgeman.

"I assure you, Miss Nightingale," said the nun crisply, "we are *not* leaving. We have come to do our duty, and we will leave when our duty to God and the British Empire has been performed—and not before. Now. May I speak to the *real* person in charge?"

Florence Nightingale turned back slowly and gazed into the combative eyes of Mother Bridgeman. "Robbie," she said quietly, tilting her chin up, "will you please inform Major Sillery that Mother Bridgeman and her volunteers are here?"

Robbie left reluctantly. Things were getting *very* interesting in the entryway to Barracks Hospital.

When he returned with an irritated and unwilling Major Sillery, Florence Nightingale and the Irish nun were still standing in the entryway sizing each other up. Florence turned to the major and said with a sudden smile, "Major Sillery, this is Mother Bridgeman. She and her...er...volunteers...are eager to assist you in your work here." Again Miss Nightingale turned to go.

"Uh, please wait, Miss Nightingale," said Major Sillery hastily, his face suddenly flushed with sweat. "You are more qualified to handle the...er...nursing staff. Please, carry on."

Robbie's eyes widened. It was the closest Major Sillery had ever come to acknowledging Miss Nightingale's official role at the hospital. The boy wanted to laugh, but tried hard to keep a straight face.

"But, Major Sillery," Florence said calmly, "you know we have absolutely no room in this hospital to sleep additional nursing staff. My own thirty-eight nurses are crammed into three small rooms. It is obvious we do not have room for—how many did you say are with you, Mother Bridgeman?"

Mother Bridgeman eyed Major Sillery. "Forty-five. Fourteen of me own Irish nuns, twenty-two nurses, and nine gentlewomen. So you see, we are prepared to offer whatever spiritual or physical comfort is needed."

Major Sillery cleared his throat but seemed unable to speak. So Florence Nightingale went on calmly, coolly, "Well, that remains to be seen. The first order of business is to find lodging for you in Scutari. As you must know, the hospital is overflowing with the sick and wounded. There is absolutely no room to lodge you here. I am afraid you will have to use your own money—you all have some means of support, I trust—to purchase housing in the town."

Again there were murmurs of dismay. "But, miss," cried one of the new volunteers, "we were told the British army would pay for our keep once we got to Turkey, in exchange for our, you know, volunteer work."

Robbie thought he heard Major Sillery groan.

"You were misinformed," said Florence. She turned to the gentlewomen in their silk dresses and fine wool cloaks. "How about you ladies?" she inquired. "You obviously have money. You must be prepared to cover the expenses of your less well-to-do sisters at this unfortunate time."

The ladies looked flustered. "But, Miss Nightingale, we—that is—well, this is quite unexpected. We are quite broke ourselves."

Florence Nightingale narrowed her eyes. "What do you mean, broke? Your families certainly did not send you on a voyage to a strange country with no money! And there is certainly no way to spend it all on board ship."

Again the gentlewomen looked flustered. "Well, you see—"

"—this is all so exciting and new that—"

"—it was such a marvelous opportunity, traveling through the Mediterranean, you see—"

"—Oh! It was so thrilling to see Madrid and Paris—"

"—and the hotels were so grand and—"

"—shopping. Wasn't shopping fun, girls?"

There was a chorus of nervous giggles.

Florence Nightingale put her hands on her hips and glared at the flock of nervous women in front of her. "You mean to tell me that you spent all your money on luxurious travel on your way here and are now penniless?! Of all the selfish—" She broke off, furious.

When she had gotten control of herself, Florence turned to the hospital commandant. "Major Sillery, who is the English Ambassador in Constantinople?"

"Lord Stratford, you mean," said the major, still looking like he wished he were someplace else.

"Exactly," said Florence. "Would you be so kind as to send a messenger that we need his help in finding housing for these...ladies. Until then, they can make themselves comfortable here in the entryway."

With that, Florence Nightingale disappeared into the hallway, leaving Mother Bridgeman and her forty-five volunteers looking around the bare entryway for something to sit on.

✧ ✧ ✧ ✧

William was not well. His leg stump had developed an infection, and he constantly had a cold and looked pale and feverish. Still, he hooted with laughter when Robbie told him about the landing of the English ladies and the Irish sisters. "This I've got to see," he chortled, grabbing his crutches and pulling himself up. "Do you think they'll be back today?"

Robbie laughed. "No doubt about it. I don't think Mother Bridgeman will be very easy to get rid of."

The boys made their way at William's pace to the nurses' quarters at the far corner of the hospital and peeked inside. Sure enough, Mother Bridgeman was seated in Miss Nightingale's office.

"Where are the Catholic soldiers?" the nun asked. "I would like to bring them some spiritual comfort."

"Mother Bridgeman," said Florence Nightingale patiently. "This is a nonsectarian hospital. The sick and wounded are not divided according to their denomination or religion. In most cases we do not even know their religious affiliation."

"You don't know?!" said Mother Bridgeman, shocked. "But—how can one possibly minister to their spiritual needs otherwise?"

Florence Nightingale looked at her calmly. "I pray for *all* of them."

Robbie thought of the whispered prayers and blessings that Miss Nightingale gave to the men on her nightly rounds at the two hospitals.

Mother Bridgeman looked at Florence with disapproval. "Well! That is quite inadequate. I see there are some things that will need to change around here."

"Hoo-eee!" William hissed in Robbie's ear. "Mother Brickbat's got her dander up."

Robbie snorted. Brickbat! It really fit. But he tried not to laugh. He wanted to hear Miss Nightingale.

"Mother Bridgeman," she was saying firmly, "we

have two well-qualified chaplains here—a military chaplain and a civilian chaplain. Any organized religious activity must be coordinated through them. As for the women who have come with you, let me remind you that I am in charge of the nursing staff here. Nurses are here to assist the doctors and aid in the comfort of the patients. We have yet to determine how we can use you—or whether we can use you at all. But whatever happens, all nurses are responsible to me and must obey my rules."

"Impossible!" sniffed Mother Bridgeman. "My nuns are responsible to no one but me."

Florence Nightingale sighed. "Then I will give my orders to you, and you can pass them along to the sisters in your charge. But we must all work as one— just as the Catholic sisters, Baptists, and Church of England nurses do under my charge already. That is why we wear a similar uniform—"

"Never!" said Mother Bridgeman.

Miss Nightingale caught Robbie's eye peeking around the doorway. With a slight smile, she moved smoothly to the door and shut it in the boys' faces.

"Whew!" said William. "Miss Nightingale's got her hands full with ol' Brickbat in there."

Robbie snickered, and soon the boys were laughing until their sides ached. "Well, I'll tell you one thing," Robbie finally said, wiping his nose with his coat sleeve, "if Miss Nightingale belongs to a religious sect, it's the sect of the Good Samaritan!"

Chapter 9

Drinking the Dead Horse

MOTHER BRIDGEMAN and her party of nuns, nurses, and "lady volunteers" were leaving—but not far. Even though Florence Nightingale had offered to send home some of the Catholic nuns among her own nurses in order to make room for some of the Irish nuns on her staff, Mother Bridgeman wouldn't hear of it. "All me nuns stay together, and I with them!" she had said stoutly.

Finally, after several weeks of wrangling, Lord Stratford, the ambassador, sent some of the women home and suggested that Mother Bridgeman and the rest of her volunteers be sent to Balaklava to give assistance to the makeshift hospitals closer to the battlefield.

Florence Nightingale wasn't entirely happy with the decision. "If efficient nursing is to ever become a reality in our military hospitals," she told the ambassador privately, "we need high nursing standards and an organized plan—not merely groups of volunteers trying to do the job a dozen different ways."

Lord Stratford was sympathetic but assured her the compromise was the best that could be done.

Now, a few weeks into the new year, 1855, Lord Stratford, Major Sillery, Florence Nightingale, and Robbie stood on the docks watching the longboats take the women to the troop ship anchored in the harbor. They were accompanied by soldiers who were being sent back to their regiments after recovering from their wounds or sickness.

Many of the soldiers had whispered words of thanks to Florence Nightingale before getting in the longboats, and they waved as the oars pulled against the tide, taking them back to the battlefield.

"I wonder if we shall see them again," she said.

"Hoo, boy, I hope not!" said Robbie, without thinking. "To me, it's good riddance to old Mother Brickbat!"

He was suddenly aware of three pairs of eyes looking at him in shocked silence. Then he felt Miss Nightingale's firm grip as she steered him away from the docks and back up the hill to the hospital.

"I was talking about the soldiers, you goose!" she said sternly. Then her voice seemed to break a little. "What—what did you call her? Mother *Brickbat*?"

Robbie nodded, bracing himself for a tongue lashing. But after a moment, he glanced at Miss Nightingale out of the corner of his eye. She was biting her lip, her shoulders shaking with silent laughter.

❖ ❖ ❖ ❖

Robbie was worried about William. It was now February, and even though it had been three months since William had lost his leg, the older boy seemed sick all the time. Even Robbie had bouts of diarrhea.

"I know, Robbie," sighed Miss Nightingale when he told her about it. "It's not just William. In spite of providing clean bedding and trying to give the men better nursing care, the death rate at the hospital is still rising. If it's not dysentery, typhoid, or cholera that kills them, it'll be scurvy."

"Have you tasted that nasty gruel the hospital cook serves the patients?" broke in Mrs. Roberts, who wasn't shy about expressing her opinions. Robbie made a face. He was sick of the brackish liquid called "soup" that was served five days out of seven.

"I have begged and begged for more nutritious food for the men," said Miss Nightingale, more to herself than to Robbie or Mrs. Roberts. "If we can't get fresh fruit and vegetables for them, any kind of citrus would help—even lemon juice or lime juice."

Robbie went cold. "Did—did you say *lime juice*?" He swallowed hard. "B-but, Miss Nightingale, there's twenty thousand pounds of lime juice stored in a shed at the dock! It's been there since December!"

❖ ❖ ❖ ❖

Robbie could hardly keep up as Florence Nightingale strode swiftly down the muddy, rutted hill toward Scutari harbor, her cloak and hood flapping in the wind. He felt miserable. This was all his fault. He had known about the lime juice, but he hadn't known it was important. It had arrived the same day the incoming wounded soldiers had been taken to Scutari General Hospital—and somehow he had forgotten about the barrels of lime juice.

The black-cloaked figure marched along the docks and into the supply office. The supply officer, sitting behind the desk with his boots up, looked startled and nearly fell off his chair trying to stand up in the presence of a lady.

"Where is the lime juice?" Florence Nightingale demanded. "I want it up at the hospital—today!"

"W-what? The lime juice? But—but there was no order for lime juice. I checked the hospital menu!"

"That's just the point," she snapped. "It's not on the menu—when it should be! Did you even consider sending word to the hospital, asking if it could be used in some way? No! And in the meantime we have men and boys dying from lack of the vitamins they need in fruit."

The flabby-faced man was trying to regain control of the situation. "We have regulations, miss," he said, stuffily. "Now if you will just bring me a supply form signed by Major Sillery—"

"Let me make myself clear," interrupted Florence sternly. "That lime juice has sat in your storehouse for three months while men are dying. I will not wait another day. I want that lime juice up at the hospital within the hour—*or I will have your job!*"

Robbie was winded by the time they had climbed back up the hill and were trying to thaw their stiff fingers by the little warming stove in Miss Nightingale's office. "It's all my fault, Miss Nightingale," he said miserably.

Florence tilted Robbie's chin and looked him in the eye. "No, it's not all your fault, Robbie. If you had told me about the lime juice last December, of course it would have been very useful. But relying on what a twelve-year-old boy just happens to see is *not* the way this is supposed to work. I have been sent here by the British government to improve the care that our wounded and sick men receive. It is my job to establish the role of nurses in improving that care. But as you know, change comes slowly to the British army, who have been doing things the same way so long, they don't know when it isn't working."

She went over to her writing desk and sat down. "Maybe it's just as well that this happened," she mused, almost to herself. "It gives me a good example of the kind of thing my nurses and I are facing here." She took out paper, ink, and a writing pen. "Robbie, can you come back here in one hour? I am going to write a letter to Sidney Herbert asking him to send me an official delegation from the War Office to evaluate the sanitary condition of this hospital. I am also going to ask him to send a new cook!"

❖ ❖ ❖ ❖

"Hey, Robbie! The lady wants you—quick like," said a soldier with his arm in a sling, poking his head into the ward Robbie and William shared with eighteen other men.

William was sick again, and Robbie spent as much time with his friend as he could. Today they were playing jackstraws on the wooden platform that served as their bed—a game that didn't use up William's low store of energy.

Robbie looked at William. Why was Miss Nightingale calling him now? He'd already run errands for her this morning—and it was hours before her nightly rounds.

William shrugged. "Better go. It's okay. I'm feeling kinda tired." He lay down listlessly, and Robbie gave him a worried look as he struggled into his military jacket and tried to button it with one hand.

Robbie made his way through the maze of hallways until he came to the nurses' quarters. Three strange gentlemen were standing in Miss Nightingale's room, dressed in neat coats-and-tails with matching waistcoats and dark trousers.

"Oh, good, Robbie, you've come," said Miss Nightingale, as he stood uncertainly in the doorway. "I want you to meet Dr. Sutherland." She indicated the oldest gentleman, a man of about sixty with muttonchop sideburns, a neat gray moustache, and a smooth-shaven chin.

"How do you do, Robbie," said the gentleman, holding out his hand.

Robbie was suddenly aware of his bandaged

stump and moved his left arm behind him as he shook hands with his right hand.

"Dr. Sutherland and these other gentlemen have come as an official Sanitary Commission to inspect Barracks Hospital," said Miss Nightingale. Robbie couldn't remember when he'd heard her sound so pleased. "But they need someone who can show them around—and no one knows the hospital like you do, Robbie. They need to see *everything*." She gave him a meaningful look.

Robbie grinned broadly. He'd show them around all right—a lot more of the hospital than they'd see if Major Sillery or one of his aides showed them around.

The tour through the wards took several hours. Dr. Sutherland said very little, but the men with him took many notes in little black notebooks. They spent a long time in the kitchen, much to the unhappiness of the hospital cook and his helpers who were trying to prepare "supper" for the hundreds of patients.

"Robbie, where does the hospital get its drinking water?" said Dr. Sutherland when the tour of the main floors of the hospital was almost over.

"Down in the basement, I think, sir. There's a cistern that collects water from several pipes...come along, I'll show you."

Robbie lit several lamps, then led the way down the rickety wooden stairs to the basement. He'd only seen the cistern once when he and William had been exploring, but he thought he could find it again. This part of the basement—separate from where the sol-

diers' wives and children were being housed—was
huge and cavernous, and it was obvious from the

straw and old piles of dung that it had been used at different times for a stable for the Turkish army when it had been an army barracks.

They found the cistern, covered by a rough wooden lid, which was half full of brackish water. Water was dribbling into the cistern from a large pipe which lay along the dirt floor and disappeared behind a crumbling wooden wall.

"Robbie, let's follow that pipe as far as we can," said Dr. Sutherland grimly.

While the men held up the lanterns, Robbie explored the wall until he found some broken boards which could be knocked to the side, creating a hole large enough for the men to crawl through. He found the pipe again, and they followed it in the gleam of the lamps. At several places the full pipe had been replaced with sections of half-pipe, like an open trough.

The smell in this part of the basement was getting worse—like something dead or decaying. Suddenly Robbie's foot hit something and he stopped. The men held up their lamps—and gasped.

There, lying over a section of the open pipe, was a big, black shape with four stiff legs, a long neck, and a big head with staring eyes. It took a minute for the scene to sink in. And then Dr. Sutherland swore quietly under his breath.

The drinking and cooking water for the entire hospital was literally passing through the partially decayed carcass of a dead horse.

Chapter 10

A Cook and a Gentleman

MAJOR SILLERY'S EYES SNAPPED FIRE. "This is highly irregular," he protested. "No one told me that a Sanitary Commission was to inspect my hospital."

"Exactly," said Dr. Sutherland dryly. "As a military man, Major, you ought to appreciate the element of *surprise* for an inspection. It provides, shall we say, a more realistic evaluation of conditions. Now, are you going to call your medical and support staff together to hear my report, or not? *Including* Miss Nightingale and her nurses."

The meeting was duly called and met in the hospital staff room behind closed doors. Robbie stationed himself near the door, trying to hear what

was going on. It wasn't hard; Dr. Sutherland had a big, booming voice, and he was angry.

"The sanitary conditions in this hospital are nothing short of *murderous*!" he thundered. There were disgruntled murmurs from within the room. "The deaths of many men who came here for healing are unnecessary and could have been prevented!"

Again murmurs arose. "You forget, Dr. Sutherland," said a sarcastic voice that sounded familiar to Robbie, "this is wartime, and we work under wartime conditions. Turkey is not merry England."

There was nervous laughter around the room.

"No, Dr. Hall," snapped Dr. Sutherland, "*you* are forgetting that Miss Nightingale, here, has pointed out time and time again the need for better sanitation, cleanliness, and nutrition. Her reports and requests have gone virtually ignored."

Robbie remembered the voice. Dr. Hall was the surgeon who had cut off his hand—without anesthetic.

"Now wait a minute, Dr. Sutherland," protested Major Sillery. "This hospital is full of sick and wounded, as you have seen for yourself. Our doctors are overworked simply caring for the most basic medical needs of wounds and disease. We hardly have time for housekeeping concerns like...like extra bedpans and scrubbing brushes."

Again the nervous laughter.

"You are wrong, Major!" thundered Dr. Sutherland's big voice. "It is those very 'housekeeping concerns,' as you call them, which create the necessary conditions for our fighting men to recover from their wounds and illnesses. You ignore them to their peril!"

Robbie couldn't hear all that went on in the meeting—but over the next few days he saw a flurry of activity all over the hospital. Turkish workmen were hired from Scutari to limewash all the walls and get rid of the rats. All the sewers were flushed with fresh water and disinfectant, and the broken water pipes replaced. All water used for drinking or cooking was boiled first. The number of slop buckets was tripled, and they were emptied twice a day.

Florence Nightingale was literally beaming. She and her nurses got down on their knees and scrubbed walls and floors, singing as they worked. Bandages were now changed daily with tender hands and motherly clucks of concern. There wasn't a ward in the hospital that Major Sillery dared to keep her out of now—even surgery.

March brought hints of spring to the sodden, muddy town of Scutari, and with it two more visitors from England: a dandy French chef named Alexis Soyer, drafted by the Secretary at War from a famous English club, and his secretary, a tall, elegant gentleman with skin as dark as a summer's night.

Robbie stared at the two men in awe. Alexis Soyer wore a blue velvet hat which slouched over one side of his head in a jaunty way. His beard was short and curly, and only covered the line of his jaw and chin, leaving his ruddy cheeks and lips free and youthful. His secretary, on the other hand, stood tall and regal, his black hair short and nappy, and he was correctly dressed, down to his button leather

gloves. *Maybe,* thought Robbie wonderingly, *he's really an African prince in disguise.*

"Why wasn't I informed of your arrival?" fumed Major Sillery, sounding like a spoiled child.

"I believe this is our introduction," said Mr. Soyer mildly, handing the hospital commandant a sealed letter. The major broke the seal and scanned the letter. Then he glanced irritably around at the little group in Miss Nightingale's office. "Well, then. Secretary at War Herbert obviously thinks you are qualified for a position as cook here in Scutari—though I hardly think a hospital resembles your fancy London club. But, orders are orders. Some of us"—he glared at Florence Nightingale—"understand the concept."

Once again Robbie was given the job of showing Alexis Soyer and his gentleman secretary—whose name was James Brandy—around the hospital, ending up in the dismal kitchen. The present cook was dismissed on the spot, the assistant cooks were immediately set to work scrubbing the big pots (which previously had been used to boil meat and make tea—without washing in between). James Brandy made a complete list of the food on hand—including several bags and barrels of food staples and spices he had brought with him from England—and Robbie was sent back to Major Sillery with a list of basic supplies which were needed immediately.

How he did it, Robbie never quite figured out, but Alexis Soyer's first meal for the thousands of patients in Barracks Hospital included fresh, home-made bread and a thick stew of lentils, dried tomatoes, carrots, potatoes, onions, and a wondrous broth.

Even William's pale face perked up when the savory stew was ladled into his bowl. "Hoo, boy," he murmured, dipping the soft bread in the broth and stuffing his mouth. And all up and down the hallways of Barracks Hospital, Robbie and William could hear soldiers in the different wards greeting the steaming pots with, "Hip, hip, hurray for the new chef!"

Florence Nightingale was delighted with the changes in the hospital menu. "It's almost like Jesus feeding the five thousand," she grinned happily to Robbie as they made their rounds one night a week later. "How does Soyer create daily miracles out of military rations for so many?"

"William looks a lot better," Robbie confided. "He hasn't had any diarrhea or stomach cramps since the drinking water was cleaned up—and I think Soyer's food is putting some color back into his face."

To his surprise, Robbie suddenly felt close to tears. He hadn't admitted, even to himself, how scared he'd been about losing William all those weeks and months when his friend was suffering one infection, cold, or illness after another. He had hardly dared to think about it, but the deep, unnamed fear was there as William had grown thinner, paler, and more listless—the same fear he'd felt all those early weeks whenever he thought of his brother Peter. But now that the danger for William seemed past—

"I think Dr. Sutherland and the Sanitary Commission saved William's life," he said in a whisper.

Florence Nightingale gave him a rough hug with one arm. "Frankly," she said, "I think they saved the whole British army!"

❖ ❖ ❖ ❖

Robbie burst into the nurses' office, but only Alexis Soyer's secretary was in the room. "Where's Miss Nightingale?" the boy asked breathlessly.

"I am wondering much the same thing," said James Brandy in his deep, refined voice. "Mr. Soyer asked me to wait here. Shall we wait together?"

"Oh," said Robbie, disappointment puckering his face. "I don't know if I can wait—see? I have a letter!" He held out a crinkled envelope. "Miss Nightingale sent me to the docks to mail her weekly report to Sidney Herbert—and an English captain gave me some letters that have come for the hospital. And... and one of them has my name on it!"

He thrust the letter in Mr. Brandy's face. The man smiled. "Why, that is so," he said. "Are you going to open it?"

Robbie looked at the toes of his boots. "I-I can recognize my name, but I can't read."

"I see," said the man. "Well, then, would you like me to read it to you?"

A grin spread over Robbie's face. He silently handed over the letter and leaned close to see the words as Mr. Brandy read.

My dear Robbie,

My heart is full of joy to know you are alive and well. Miss Nightingale has written to me three times to let me know how you are doing. She says you are being a great help to her. That makes my heart glad, though I am not surprised, for my sons have always done their duty and supported their father and me.

Your sister Margo is a hard worker, and I thank God for good health and enough work to get us by. The little ones are fine, but they miss their big brother.

As for the loss of your hand, I am sorry, my son— but as you are already discovering, it is only an obstacle to overcome, not the end of the road. As for the loss of your brother Peter—words cannot express my sorrow. But we must go on.

I look forward to your return home. But your absence is eased knowing you are safe and useful to Miss Nightingale. Stay as long as you are needed.

> *Your loving mother,*
> *Sally Robinson.*

James Brandy folded the letter and handed it back to Robbie. "Your mama sounds like a fine woman," he said warmly. "You must be proud."

Robbie nodded, a lump in his throat. "But William—he's my friend—he will never get a letter like this. He...he has no mama, you see." Robbie turned to go, but was stopped by the rich voice.

"Would you like me to teach you how to read, Robbie?" James Brandy asked.

Robbie turned back slowly, surprise lighting up his eyes. He was just about to say, "Oh yes, *please*, Mr. Brandy!" but just then Florence Nightingale, Alexis Soyer, and Major Sillery all marched into the room in the middle of a conversation.

"The army regulations state 'meat per person,'"

Alexis Soyer was saying urgently. "But it comes to me divided only by weight—so that some men get meat, while others get only fat, gristle, and bone!"

"Exactly what are you proposing, Mr. Soyer?" said Major Sillery wearily.

"Here, my secretary has it all written out," said the chef, motioning toward James Brandy, who produced a folded piece of paper from his satchel. "Read it, would you please, Mr. Brandy?"

James Brandy opened the paper and read, "All meat used for hospital patients should be de-boned, removing all fat, gristle, and bone, and then weighed to produce the required amount of 'meat per person.'"

All eyes turned to Major Sillery. The major cleared his throat. "Well-meaning, I am sure. But revising the policy would mean a new Regulation of Service, going through official army channels, to pre-bone the meat."

"And when can that happen, Major?" demanded Florence Nightingale.

Major Sillery looked her straight in the eye. "When the war is over," he said firmly and then was gone.

Florence Nightingale looked around the room. "Well, gentlemen," she sighed, "now you see what we are up against. But don't lose heart. We must think beyond this hospital, these men, this war. What we are learning here in the Crimea will be invaluable in creating reforms when the war is over. So I think I can say with St. Peter, 'Lord, it is good for us to be here'...though at times I wonder if St. Peter were here, if he would say so!"

Chapter 11

Back to Balaklava

FLORENCE NIGHTINGALE LOOKED EXHAUSTED. Robbie was worried about the dark circles under her eyes and how thin she'd gotten. But, if anything, the smile on her face seemed to be even more cheerful.

"Six months we've been here, Robbie Robinson," she said toward the end of April as they walked back from Scutari General Hospital one night, "and the patients are *finally* receiving decent treatment from the moment they arrive at our door. Why, a ship arrived just last week from the Crimea with two hundred sick and wounded. And they all were bathed, had their hair cut and washed, were given clean clothes and blankets, and were examined within the first twelve hours."

Robbie nodded in agreement. Barracks Hospital seemed like a totally different place from the evil-smelling pit he remembered that horrible day last November when the H.M.S. *Andes* landed with its load of dead and dying from the Battle of Balaklava.

"Maybe you could take a break—a little holiday," he suggested hopefully. How any woman could keep the kind of schedule Miss Nightingale kept—nursing all day, making rounds of two hospitals, then writing letters and reports until sometimes three in the morning—was beyond his understanding.

"A holiday?" She forced a laugh. "Well, I *am* planning on taking a little trip—but it is hardly a holiday I'm thinking of," she said, her voice sobering. "On May second, 420 of our brave patients are sailing once more for Balaklava, returning to the war to be shot at, sliced with a sword, or infected with cholera—whichever comes first."

They walked in silence for a few moments, then she went on. "I would like to accompany them back to their active duties—and besides, I have received permission from the Secretary at War to inspect the field hospitals at Balaklava and make recommendations for their improvement. He has given me the official title of 'Superintendent of Female Nurses in the English Military.'" She suddenly grinned and turned teasing eyes on Robbie. "Would you like to go along? I can always use my 'right-hand man'—and besides, you might get to see Mother Bridgeman again!"

Robbie rolled his eyes in mock despair.

But a few days later, on the second day of May, he was standing on the deck of the *Robert Lowe* with Florence Nightingale, watching as Mrs. Roberts, Alexis Soyer, and James Brandy also climbed aboard along with the hundreds of returning soldiers.

"Humph!" muttered Mrs. Roberts, shaking out her rumpled gray skirts after the awkward climb up the rope ladder from the longboat below. "I heard tell this boat is nicknamed the 'Robert Slow.' Mercy, mercy, how I got talked into taking this foolish sea voyage, straight into the mouth of war, I'll never know...." The motherly nurse bustled off, muttering something about "seasickness" and "stomach tea."

Robbie caught an amused gleam in Florence Nightingale's eye. They both knew Mrs. Roberts wouldn't hear of staying behind. She was the most experienced nurse on the staff at Barracks Hospital, and Florence often relied on her common sense advice. The day-to-day nursing operations back in Scutari had been left in the capable hands of Sister Alice, who accepted the responsibility with something close to missionary zeal.

Florence Nightingale also insisted on bringing Alexis Soyer and his secretary, certain now that healthy food for soldiers on active duty also needed to be number one on the list of military reforms.

It was hard for Robbie to say good-bye to William. Maybe, he thought regretfully, he should have stayed behind. He couldn't help but remember the agonizing ten-day voyage across the stormy Black Sea six months earlier, with William barely hanging on between life and death. Did he really want to go back to Balaklava—where Peter was buried?

To everyone's surprise, the spring winds were steady and strong, and the "Robert Slow" sailed into Balaklava Harbor on May 5 after only three days on the Black Sea. The returning soldiers disembarked, while the captain invited Miss Nightingale to use his ship as her headquarters while in Balaklava. She sent word to Lord Raglan, the British commander, that she would like to call on him, but he was away inspecting his troops farther inland that day. "Then," she said, "I would like to see where our good men are holding the line against Sebastapol."

By the time Miss Nightingale's party was rowed to shore, word of her arrival had spread throughout the camps. A military escort brought horses, and Florence Nightingale was given a pretty mare, which she rode sidesaddle with an easy grace. Robbie remembered seeing the Nightingale girls riding horseback around the Embley estate in their expensive riding habits...but that seemed a lifetime ago.

As the rather large party of civilians and officers rode through Balaklava and up the road toward Sebastapol, soldiers who had been at Barracks Hospital under her care and others who had only heard the stories about her came running.

"God bless you, miss!" cried one soldier with great emotion. "You're an angel."

"Aye!" cried another. "The Angel of the Crimea!"

The cry went up and down the camps. "It's the Angel of the Crimea!"

Robbie was glad they had something specific to do—he could put off thinking about the graves back in Balaklava. And he had to admit that he enjoyed the fresh spring air up on the heights as their horses jogged easily toward the Russian fortress.

When they reached their destination, the men who were manning the big guns pointing toward Sebastapol or crouched in the trenches which had been dug all around the Allied position had already heard that Miss Nightingale was coming. "Hip, hip, hurray! Hip, hip, hurray!" they cheered again and again.

She dismounted from her pretty mare and talked to the men. "What do you eat and drink every day?" she questioned. "How do you cook it?" She was appalled to discover that most of the men ate their food rations cold, sometimes even raw, because they had no fuel or camp stoves. Hot tea and coffee were almost nonexistent luxuries, even during the winter.

"Hmm," said Alexis Soyer, getting out his black notebook. He began making sketches. "I think a small, portable camp stove could be invented which would..." His voice trailed off, and for the rest of the day he and James Brandy had their heads together working on his new idea.

By the time they rode back to the ship, Florence's face was flushed and her eyes bright. "It's just all this unaccustomed fresh air," she said, brushing off Mrs. Roberts' searching eye.

The next day the inspections of the field hospitals began. At Balaklava General Hospital, the "Nightingale party" was met at the door by Dr. John Hall, who had been transferred from Scutari to Balaklava. "Good day, Dr. Hall," Florence said politely, looking her old foe in the eye. "We have come to inspect the hospitals in Balaklava. I am especially interested in seeing how the nursing staff is organized, and whether their skills are being used to the best advantage."

"By what authority?" Dr. Hall asked coolly.

Florence handed him the official letter from Sidney Herbert. Dr. Hall scanned it, then handed it back. "This says you have been named Superintendent of Female Nurses in the English Military *in Turkey*," he said triumphantly. "I hardly think this applies to the Crimea."

For a moment, Florence Nightingale looked flustered. Then she tilted her chin firmly and said, "You can fight me, Dr. Hall, or you can cooperate with me. Either way, I *will* hold this inspection, and I *do* have the authority from the Secretary at War."

The inspection was depressing. Even Robbie could see that the hospital was dirty, the nurses were idle and flirting with the military staff, basic supplies were missing, while other luxuries—such as tablecloths and silver candlesticks in the staff dining room—showed a wasteful extravagance.

As they made their rounds in the second hospital—called The Sanatorium—Robbie saw a little boy, only about five or six, wide-eyed and frightened, his head wrapped in bandages. "Hello," Robbie said, stopping beside his straw mat. "What is your name?"

The little boy only stared at him.

The others had started to move on, but Robbie hesitated. The boy was so little—too little to be a drummer boy or bugler. Why was he here? Where were his mother and father? Robbie remembered all too well how lonely and afraid he'd felt so far from home—until he met Miss Nightingale.

"Well!" said a strangely familiar, stuffy voice from the doorway. "I'd just as soon see the Queen of England as see *you*."

Robbie glanced up. There stood Mother Bridgeman in her long black veil and robe, looking disapprovingly at Florence Nightingale and her party.

"Good day, Mother Bridgeman," said Florence politely. "We have come—"

"I know why you have come. To poke your nose in me business, that's what. Well, go on—the sooner you do it, the sooner you'll be gone." The nun turned to go.

"Wait!" said Robbie, surprising himself. "This little boy—who is he?"

"The enemy, that's who," said Mother Bridgeman irritably. "Russian boy...an orphan. Name's Peter Grillage. Got hurt in the shelling, then dumped on our doorstep to care for. And taking up good bed space, too," she huffed. She turned grandly and disappeared.

Robbie couldn't stop thinking about the little Russian boy as they toured the third "hospital"—which was really a collection of huts up on the heights overlooking Balaklava, called Castle Hospital. What was going to happen to him?

Back on board ship that night, Florence, Mrs. Roberts, Alexis Soyer, and James Brandy talked long into the night, devising plans for new hospital kitchens. Some of the so-called nurses definitely had to go, Florence told the others; they were incompetent, rude, and she smelled alcohol on their breath. "However," she went on, "the head nurse at Castle Hospital—Mrs. Stewart, a decent woman—confided to me that Dr. Hall makes her life difficult. I must talk to her more tomorrow."

But as Robbie fell asleep with their voices droning in the background, his mind could think of only one thing: little Peter Grillage's frightened face.

✧ ✧ ✧ ✧

Heavy rain during the night turned Balaklava into a mud bath. It was still drizzling when Florence Nightingale and her companions were rowed to shore, crowded as best they could under two big black umbrellas. Robbie hunched his shoulders gloomily. He had wanted to go looking today for the place his brother was buried, but his hopes were evaporating. Not in this weather.

The party stopped at The Sanatorium first so that Miss Nightingale and Alexis Soyer could discuss plans for a new kitchen with the hospital military commandant. While the grown-ups were dickering over the details, Robbie slipped away unnoticed. Keeping a sharp eye out for Mother Bridgeman, he made his way through the wards until he found little Peter Grillage again, huddled under a thin, dirty army blanket.

"Hey," said Robbie, smiling.

The boy just stared, his eyes wild and afraid.

Robbie squatted down and gently pulled back the blanket. The boy was shirtless, and his ribs stood out from his thin chest. Dirt matted the dark hair that stuck out from beneath the bandage around his head. But other than the head wound and a mess of bruises and scratches over his body, the boy did not seem to have any major injuries.

Robbie reached out and touched the boy's shoulder. Peter shrank back from the touch. "It's okay," Robbie crooned. "I won't hurt you." He covered the little boy with the smelly blanket, but as he turned to go, he felt small fingers suddenly grasp his hand, as if begging him to stay.

Nervous that Mother Bridgeman might find him there, Robbie shook his head. "But I'll be back," he grinned.

The meeting was just breaking up as Robbie slipped back into the room. No one seemed to have missed him. "Then it's agreed," Florence Nightingale was saying. "Mr. Soyer will be glad to train the hospital cooks in proper nutrition, but—" Her voice faltered. "But there must be..."

Everyone looked at her sharply as her voice trailed off once more. Her hand went uncertainly to her face, which was flushed unnaturally, and small wisps of damp curls escaped from under her trim cap.

And then suddenly Florence Nightingale crumpled in a heap on the floor.

Chapter 12

The Trick That Failed

SHE'S GOT CRIMEAN FEVER," Dr. Hall pronounced grimly, straightening up after his examination. The senior medical officer had been quickly summoned from Balaklava General Hospital, while Mrs. Roberts anxiously fanned Florence Nightingale where she lay on the floor.

"Whatever that is," muttered Soyer under his breath. The French cook had a steadying grip on Robbie's shoulders, whose legs seemed to have turned to jelly.

"Miss Nightingale's quarters must be moved from the ship in the harbor immediately," Dr. Hall went on briskly, "and she must be taken to Castle Hospital where she can get some fresh air. Can you men carry her up there?"

Robbie wanted to cry out, "I will help carry!"—but he just stared stupidly at his missing left hand. Even if he were a grown man, he could not carry the stretcher on which his friend now lay.

The rain was still coming down as Alexis Soyer and James Brandy lifted the unconscious woman and eased her out the door. "The umbrella!" Soyer shouted. "Shield her with the umbrella!"

Robbie grabbed James Brandy's big black umbrella and struggled fiercely to open it with his one good hand. As he struggled, Mrs. Roberts gently took it from him, shook out the umbrella, and held it over Florence Nightingale as the procession wound its way up the muddy road to the hospital huts on the heights. Robbie trudged behind in misery.

Florence was soon stripped of her wet clothing and put to bed in one of the hospital huts. Mrs. Stewart, the head nurse, was assigned to her care. She immediately took charge. "Out," she ordered briskly. "Everybody out! You will not help her by hovering like so many mournful hound dogs. Go on now and come back tomorrow!"

Mrs. Roberts started to protest, but Alexis Soyer and James Brandy each took her by an arm and guided her back to the harbor to pack up Miss Nightingale's things. No one noticed that Robbie parked himself just outside the hut on the small, sheltered stoop, his knees drawn up and tightly clasped by his arms. Hours passed, and still Robbie kept vigil.

"Robbie Robinson? Is that you?"

As if in a dream, Robbie looked up into the whiskered face of William Russell of the *London Times*.

"Word got around quickly about Miss Nightingale's sudden illness," said the reporter, putting one foot on the stoop and resting an elbow on his knee. "I just returned with Lord Raglan to find all the camps clear up to Sebastapol talking of nothing else! Can you tell me what happened? How is she?"

Robbie just stared blankly at the man for several moments. "I said I would always be her man!" he finally whispered fiercely. "But...I couldn't help carry her and...and I'm not tall enough to hold the umbrella." Tears finally slid down his face, unbidden.

✧ ✧ ✧ ✧

Day after day Florence Nightingale battled a raging fever, slipping in and out of unconsciousness.

The second day the rain had stopped, and Mr. Russell took Robbie to the place where he'd helped bury the dead after the Battle of Balaklava and the charge of the Light Brigade. No gravestone marked the place—just a field of rough ground, with weeds and wildflowers growing from the rocky soil.

Robbie stood silently as a light breeze ruffled his shaggy hair. What a fine sight Peter had been in his blue uniform of the Seventeenth Lancers, sitting proudly in the saddle as Wolfgang pranced beneath him, wearing that cocky smile. Yes, that is how he would remember Peter.

He turned quickly and started back toward Balaklava. "There's another Peter who needs me now," he said abruptly to the man from the *London Times*.

While Florence Nightingale fought her battle with Crimean Fever, Robbie divided his time between keeping vigil at the door of her hut and sneaking into The Sanatorium to see little Peter Grillage. The Russian boy's eyes gradually lost their scared-rabbit look, and his face lit up whenever Robbie appeared. Soon they were able to communicate with sign language and a few basic English words.

"Eat!" Robbie urged, bringing him some fresh bread that Soyer had baked.

"Shirt," he said, pulling a too-large but clean, warm shirt that he'd smuggled out of army supplies over Peter's head and arms.

"Shhh. Don't tell Mother Brickbat," he always whispered before he snuck out once more.

One afternoon, when the warm May sun was finally beginning to dry up the mud, Robbie watched several British soldiers come up the road and make their way to Miss Nightingale's hut. One of the soldiers was carrying a big, wiggly, black dog.

"It's a present from the soldiers to our dear lady," the soldiers announced to an astonished Mrs. Roberts, who met them at the door. "A fine puppy—we all chipped in and bought it for Miss Nightingale."

"Of all the—!" said a flustered Mrs. Roberts. "Why, you'll do no such thing! Take it away—go on now. Shoo! Shoo!" And she flapped her apron at them .

The soldiers laughed and backed off as the door slammed in their faces. But a few moments later the soldier with the dog under his arm ambled back and cocked a finger at Robbie. "From the Sixty-Eighth, aren't ya, lad?" he said, grinning, nodding at Robbie's uniform jacket. "You're our man...here." And he dumped the warm, wiggling dog into Robbie's arms. "Take care of it for her, will ya, lad? And when she's better, give it to her with the soldiers' love."

✧ ✧ ✧ ✧

With Mrs. Roberts staying with Florence Nightingale night and day in the hospital hut on the heights, it wasn't too hard to hide the dog from her. But Robbie had to bring Alexis Soyer and James Brandy in on the conspiracy.

"The responsibility is all yours, boy," said Soyer mildly. "But we'll keep your secret. The pup can bunk here with us, and no one will be the wiser."

The two men and the former drummer boy had been given a tent in one of the camps just outside Balaklava. While they waited for word on Florence Nightingale's condition, Soyer tried his best to improve the diets of the patients in the three hospitals, battling the slow machinery of "army regulations." He also spent his evenings working on his new invention—a portable camp stove that could be shared by two or three soldiers out in the field.

Robbie felt a little guilty as the puppy dove under his blanket each night, washing Robbie's face with his pink tongue. This was Miss Nightingale's dog, not his. He shouldn't get too attached. But morning always found Robbie and the pup snuggled together in a heap of arms, legs, and soft fur.

After two long, anxious weeks, Florence Nightingale's fever finally broke, leaving her weak but alert. Still, Mrs. Roberts and Mrs. Stewart were fiercely protective, only allowing the doctors in and keeping visitors out. Robbie still kept up his vigil outside her door, so he watched with interest one afternoon as two riders came up the road toward Castle Hospital. Even at a distance he could see that the older gentleman in a decorated military uniform had one loose sleeve tucked in his belt.

"Lord Raglan, sir!" said Robbie, and scrambled to hold the fine horse as the general dismounted.

Mrs. Roberts almost didn't let the general come in, but he insisted and stayed quite a while. When the door finally opened, Robbie heard him say, "All of England will be glad to know you are still alive and kicking, Miss Nightingale. Even the Queen of England has been waiting for some good news about your recovery. I shall send a telegram tonight."

Once outside, Lord Raglan spoke soberly to Mrs. Robert. "If I could, I would send her home to England immediately, but she will have none of it. The best I can do is insist that she return to Scutari for six weeks of complete rest—and not in Barracks Hospital, either! I will ask Dr. Hall to make arrangements for your party to sail with the first available ship— but the rest is up to you."

✧ ✧ ✧

Florence Nightingale was not at all happy about returning to Scutari. "Why, we have not yet accomplished what we came here to do!" she complained to Alexis Soyer. "The nurses are still unorganized, and your kitchen reforms have not been acted upon." But for once in her life she was too weak to insist, and plans were made for her to sail on the *Jura*.

On the appointed day, Florence Nightingale was brought down to the harbor in a borrowed carriage, attended by Alexis Soyer and Mrs. Roberts. Unlike most of the ships, which were anchored out in the harbor, the *Jura* was tied up to the docks, making it easier to bring the sick woman on board.

"Mr. Brandy," Robbie said, pulling Soyer's secretary aside. "Would you take the pup and...and give it to Miss Nightingale when Mrs. Roberts can't make a fuss?" He thrust the short rope tied to a leather strap around the dog's neck into James Brandy's hand.

Brandy frowned. "Why me? What are you going to do?" he asked suspiciously.

"I-I got something to do. Don't let the ship sail without me!" With that Robbie took off at a run, heading straight for The Sanatorium.

The nurses and medics were used to seeing the drummer boy around the hospital, but Robbie walked through the hallways carefully. He didn't want to run into Mother Bridgeman by accident.

Slipping unnoticed into the ward, Robbie bent over Peter Grillage's bed. "Come on," he whispered, putting a finger to his lips. He crouched next to the straw mat, and with his right hand scooped Peter

onto his back. The little boy was surprisingly light. To Robbie's relief, the boy didn't make a sound but clung tightly to Robbie's neck as the older boy trotted anxiously back through the hallways.

A nurse stared at them suspiciously. "Just giving the little guy a bit of exercise," Robbie called out to her brightly. She shrugged and turned, and Robbie slipped into the next hall and out a side door.

Over and over Robbie rehearsed what he was going to say to Miss Nightingale when they got to the ship. "He hasn't got any folks, you see—and Mother Brickbat doesn't like him. Calls him 'the enemy.' What's going to happen to him here? At least in Scutari we can look after him, and—"

By now Robbie had a pain in his side, and Peter's grip on his coat was beginning to slip. He lowered the boy to the ground and, holding Peter's hand, walked the last short distance to the docks.

As the two boys neared the *Jura*, a military messenger sprinted past them and hailed one of the crewmen. "Hey, there," panted the messenger, "I'm supposed to give these letters to the captain of the ship sailing for Scutari—would that be the *Jura*?"

"Sorry, mate," grunted the crewman, hefting the heavy ropes that bound the ship to the dock. "The *Jura*'s not putting in at Scutari—we're heading straight for England."

Robbie stopped short, dumbfounded. Did he hear the man right? *Not* putting in at Scutari—

Suddenly, he grabbed Peter in his arms and dashed frantically up the gangplank. "Mr. Soyer!" he yelled. "Mr. Brandy! Get Miss Nightingale off this ship immediately! We've been tricked!"

Chapter 13

The Spoils of War

YOU MEAN," said William in disbelief, "Dr. Hall actually tried to *trick* Miss Nightingale by getting passage for her on a ship that wasn't even headed for Scutari?"

Robbie was trying to fill William in on what all had happened on their trip to Balaklava. The two boys were sitting against a gravestone in the graveyard near Barracks Hospital on top of the hill over-

looking Scutari. In the distance, across the Strait of Bosporus, they could see the tall minarets stabbing the air above the sprawling city of Constantinople. Nearby Peter Grillage, squealing with glee, was playing a game of chase between the gravestones with Rousch, the big, black puppy.

"Yep!" said Robbie. "Guess Dr. Hall saw this as his chance to get rid of Miss Nightingale and her 'meddling' with the army hospitals. Probably thought she'd be too sick to ask where the ship was headed. Would've worked, too, if I hadn't overhead the sailor say the *Jura* was heading straight for England."

William threw one of his crutches into the air and laughed as it somersaulted back to earth. "Hoo, boy! I sure would have liked to see Dr. Hall's face when he discovered his trick didn't work!" Then he cocked his head at Robbie. "Say—what happened then? And what did Miss Nightingale say about you stealing Peter right out from under Mother Brickbat's nose?"

Robbie shrugged and grinned. "There was so much confusion and commotion getting Miss Nightingale and all the baggage off the ship, and trying to find a transport heading for Scutari, that nobody really noticed for a while that we had an extra passenger. Mr. Soyer found a private yacht belonging to some British nobleman—Lord Ward, I think his name was—who was so upset that Miss Nightingale had been treated this way, that he offered to have his captain sail her across the Black Sea in his own ship...and here we are!"

William scowled. "Come on—tell me what happened. You're leaving stuff out."

"Well, nothing much, really," said Robbie, idly picking a daisy-like wildflower from the ragged grass between the gravestones. "Peter and I kinda lay low in the stern of the yacht with Rousch till we were well out of the Balaklava harbor. Miss Nightingale was pretty bad off with all the stress and excitement happening so soon after her fever, so everybody was fussing around her in the captain's cabin. But finally James Brandy came lookin' for me, and when he saw Peter he figured out what I'd done. But he didn't say much. He just shook his head, rolled his eyes heavenward, and—say! Did I tell you that he's teaching me to read?"

"Robbie Robinson!" shouted William, cuffing Robbie on the arm so hard he fell over. "You can be so maddening! What—did—Miss—Nightingale—say?!"

"All right, all right!" said Robbie, picking himself up with mock wounded dignity and leaning against the gravestone once more. "I have to admit, I thought she might be mad—you know how she is, trying to work within the system, even when it means her reforms go a lot slower. So I thought I'd get a lecture saying I should have asked for permission to take Peter with us, on and on...but it was funny. When Mr. Soyer and Mr. Brandy finally presented us to her in her cabin, she just looked at Peter a long time, then lifted him up onto her bed and said to herself, 'I guess after any battle, the spoils of war go to the victor.' Now, what do you think she meant by that?"

✧ ✧ ✧ ✧

"She's coming! She's coming!" squealed one of the

132

nurses. There was a flurry of gray skirts and white aprons as the nurses lined themselves up in presentable order. Robbie and William were also on hand for Miss Nightingale's return, and Peter Grillage had been scrubbed to rosy perfection by Mrs. Roberts.

Florence Nightingale had been recuperating from her severe illness at the house of Mr. Sabin, the hospital chaplain, in Scutari. She had kept Rousch, the dog, with her for company, but Peter had stayed at the hospital in the motherly care of Mrs. Roberts—except it was Robbie and William who took him out into the fresh air each day, and made up games to keep him entertained when Mrs. Roberts had to be on duty.

Robbie had seen Miss Nightingale several times during her recovery—stopping by the house to exercise the dog or to take some letters down to the docks for her. But she'd been shielded from the day-to-day operations at Barracks Hospital in order for her to get complete rest.

As she walked into the room after her six weeks of enforced rest, there was a small gasp from several of the nurses. She was much thinner, and her hair, which had been cropped short during her fever, was growing in soft, girlish curls. Her dark eyes looked huge in her pale face.

"Welcome back, Miss Nightingale!" said Mrs. Roberts warmly, accompanied by a chorus of greetings.

Florence smiled graciously, then looked around the group. "Some of the nurses are missing," she said slowly. "Where is Katie Black and...Betsy Horn?"

Sister Alice stepped forward. "I'm sorry to report that Miss Black and Miss Horn were feeling rather dandy one night while you were in Balaklava and... well, I had to dismiss them for getting drunk with some of the soldiers."

A shadow passed over Florence's eyes. "You were quite right to do so, Sister Alice. They knew the rules."

"Thank you, Miss Nightingale!" said Sister Alice, relief flushing the anxiety from her face. Standing in for Florence Nightingale had been more than the Catholic sister had bargained for, but the nursing superintendent's praise lifted the burden she'd been carrying.

Another nurse stepped forward, young, pretty... and nervous. She cleared her throat and handed Florence a folded piece of paper. "It-it's me resignation, Miss Nightingale," she stammered. Then she blushed. "I'm getting married in a fortnight."

Five more nurses stepped forward, each handing Miss Nightingale their resignations.

The first nurse cleared her throat again. "We know it's against the rules to get married while on a tour of duty, so we want to give you proper notice."

"It's not because we're unhappy with the nursing, miss," spoke one of the other brides-to-be. "Oh, no. We've learned ever so much. It's just that... well," she giggled nervously, "you know how love is."

Miss Nightingale did not look amused. "Yes, I know how love is. It can distract us from our duty and keep us from our calling. Nonetheless, what's done is done. I accept your resignations and thank you for your service."

All the nurses except Mrs. Roberts filed out, and Florence sank into a hard-backed chair wearily. Then she smiled at the three boys standing like stairsteps before her: William, now seventeen and tall, filling out like a man, even while standing on one leg and two makeshift crutches; Robbie, a head shorter at thirteen, in robust good health except for his missing left hand; and Peter, six years old, his round cherubic face dimpled with pleasure, even if he didn't understand everything that was going on.

"My boys," she murmured. "Whatever is to become of you?"

She gave them each a hug and some Turkish sweets she'd picked up in the Scutari market. "Now, Mrs. Roberts," she said briskly, shooing the boys out the door, "let's get down to business. I need a full report on the state of things at Barracks Hospital."

Peter tugged on Robbie's sleeve; he wanted to go outside and eat his sweets. Robbie shook his head; Miss Nightingale might need him to run errands or take messages. She still didn't have her full strength back. William shrugged good-naturedly. "I'll look after him," he said, and swung after the little boy on his crutches.

Behind the half-open door Mrs. Roberts was saying, "Unfortunately, many of the hospital personnel have been reassigned. Major Sillery is gone, and so are many of the doctors—and their replacements seem totally ignorant of what we've been trying to do! I daresay, some days it seems like we might as well pack up and go home!"

There was a brief silence. Then Miss Nightingale spoke. "Nay, Mrs. Roberts. To give less than every ounce of strength would not be enough—would not be what God expects of me. For God is the only master I acknowledge; I am His representative here at Scutari; the work I do is His work. That is all the reward, all the encouragement, I need. If the work is not yet done, we must simply keep praying, 'Lord, Your will be done.'"

❖ ❖ ❖ ❖

Summer had turned to fall when the new hospital commandant received the telegram on September 9, 1855, from Balaklava. Its contents spread like wildfire through all the wards at Barracks Hospital.

Sebastapol has fallen 8 September. Victory is within our grasp.

"The war is as good as over," said William soberly. Cheers were ringing up and down the halls, but the older boy didn't smile.

"Ain't you happy?" said Robbie. "We can go home now!"

William swallowed. "That's just it. I ain't got a home to go to. This"—his eyes swept the limewashed stone walls of the hospital—"has been home for me. With you...and Miss Nightingale...and little Peter."

Robbie just stared at his friend. He didn't know what to say.

✧ ✧ ✧ ✧

It was months before the Allies pulled out of the Crimea. Once again, British troop ships sailed the Mediterranean with their load of soldiers and cavalry horses—but thousands had been left behind in unmarked graves in a strange land.

Spring was budding again, 1856, when the hired cart rumbled down the lane toward the village of Wellow. "My village is up ahead," said Robbie to his

companions, excitement rising up in his throat. "But this is Embley—your new home."

The carter pulled up his mule before the wide, pretty drive leading up to the big Nightingale house. Little Peter and the big, black dog scrambled out willy-nilly, while William carefully got himself balanced on his crutches. Slowly, the strange-looking quartet made their way up the drive, up the steps to the wide verandah, and were just about to lift the door knocker when the door opened wide.

"Oh, Mama!" said the astonished young woman with dark hair who had opened the door. "They're here—the orphans Flo wrote about! And...and the Robinson boy."

"Oh, my," said another voice, and a handsome older woman joined her daughter at the door. Robbie recognized them as Florence Nightingale's mother and sister, Parthenope. "I-I...well...oh, my. I guess you better come in. Uh, Edwin! Could you please take the dog to...er...the stable, I guess, for now."

Robbie reluctantly let the stern-looking butler take Rousch's rope and followed the two women into the lavish house. He knew Rousch wouldn't stay in the stable for long—not if Miss Nightingale had anything to say about it. For a year now the dog had slept every night on the floor right beside her cot in the nurses' office.

"But where is Florence?" asked Mrs. Nightingale, who still seemed to be in shock at the appearance of the three boys. She kept staring at William's missing leg and Robbie's left arm. "We thought surely she would arrive first to explain—I mean, news about her adoption of...is it William? and little Peter, here...has taken us all *quite* by surprise."

"I'm sure she'll be home in a day or two, ma'am," said Robbie politely. "She didn't come home on a troop ship because she wanted to avoid a lot of fuss and publicity when she arrived."

"Avoid a fuss!" exclaimed Parthenope with a nervous laugh. "Not much chance of that, I'm afraid. Her friends at the War Office have taken her reports from the Crimea very much to heart, and there's talk everywhere about her reforms. Why, just before Christmas there was a big social gala—wasn't it grand, Mama?—for the sole purpose of raising money for a medical school to train *decent* nurses!"

The emphasis was on "decent," and Robbie remembered Miss Nightingale's war to change the common opinion of nurses as "loose women."

"The 'Nightingale Fund' they call it," Parthenope chattered on. "They're just waiting for her to get back to England to help raise more money—by speaking, and things like that."

"Hoo, boy," said William under his breath to Robbie. "Is that good news or bad news?"

Just then a maid came into the room. "Will the, er, visitors be staying for tea, madam?"

"Why—yes, of course. Oh, my," said Mrs. Nightingale, quite flustered. "I have forgotten my manners. All three of you must be very hungry and thirsty after your journey."

Peter attacked the fresh-squeezed lemonade,

cakes, bread, and butter with gusto, his grin wide and his cheeks rosy. Already Robbie could see that the nervous Parthenope was charmed by the little boy. William, on the other hand, seemed uncomfortable and kept glancing about, as if looking for an escape hatch.

When tea was finished, Robbie cleared his throat and said he must be going. "My mama and Margo and the little ones will be wanting to know I'm back," he said. "I don't know if they got my letter saying when I'd be coming." Robbie couldn't help the note of pride that crept into his voice when he said "my letter." His mama would be so surprised and pleased to see that he could read and write!

Robbie gave Peter Grillage a playful hug, then turned to William. "It'll be all right when Miss Nightingale gets here," he whispered to his friend. "Besides, I live right down the road—I'll come by every day to see you."

"Promise?" William whispered back fiercely.

"Promise," Robbie grinned.

Robbie could see his two friends standing on the Nightingale verandah waving at him until the road to Wellow took him out of their sight. Then he hoisted his pack and speeded up his steps. Things would be different now...without Papa...without his brother Peter. Without his hand.

But he was going home.

More About Florence Nightingale

TWO BABY GIRLS WERE BORN to William (W.E.N.) and Fanny Nightingale on an extended trip in Europe. Parthenope, the first, was born in Naples, Greece. The second was named after the Italian city in which she was born on May 12, 1820: Florence.

Florence Nightingale grew up in a wealthy family on the outskirts of London in a whirl of parties, a summer home named Lea Hurst, and trips to Europe. But in 1837, at the age of sixteen, she wrote in her diary: "On February 7 God spoke to me and called me to His service." But what service?

She discovered that she felt energized and fulfilled—not by the "society" of wealthy families —but when she was nursing the poor families in the "cottages" around Embley, the family home.

By the time Florence was twenty-four years old, she was certain that her calling was caring for the sick. But in the 1840s, proper English girls weren't nurses. Nurses were nothing more than maids-of-all-work in common hospitals (the rich were cared for at home), and said to be drunkards or prostitutes.

By now, Florence, unmarried and still living with her parents, was nearly going mad with enforced idleness and frustration. She asked a visiting American physician, Dr. Samuel Howe, "Would it be unsuitable for an English girl to devote her life to nursing?" He replied, "In England, whatever is unusual is thought to be unsuitable. But there is never anything unbecoming or unladylike in doing your duty for the good of others."

Florence wondered why the Protestant church had nothing similar to the Catholic Sisters of Charity—a way for women to spend their life serving others. Dr. Howe told her about Kaiserworth in Germany, established by Pastor Theodor Fliedner, which included a hospital with a hundred beds, an infant school, a penitentiary with twelve inmates, an orphan asylum, a school for training teachers, and a training school for nurses with a hundred deaconnesses. Everything was accompanied by prayer.

Even before visiting, Florence's spirit responded deeply: Kaiserworth was her destiny.

In 1846, Florence took a trip to Rome with friends Charles and Selina Bracebridge. On this trip she met Sidney Herbert and his wife Liz, who were devout Christians. He later became Secretary at War and a friend and supporter of Florence Nightingale.

In July of 1850, at the age of thirty, Florence finally went to Kaiserworth in Germany for two weeks. A year later she returned for three months. She went home with a new attitude: now she knew she was going to escape her restricted life.

Three years later she took her first nursing job, as superintendent at the "Institution for the Care for Sick Gentlewomen in Distressed Circumstances." She moved the institution to new premises and established several revolutionary ideas: having hot water piped to every floor; a lift to bring up patients' food; and patients able to ring for the nurse directly. She was also determined that the Institution be "nonsectarian"—would take in all denominations and religions as patients. (Her committee wanted it to be only for members of the Church of England.)

In March 1854, when England and France declared war on Russia for control of the Crimea and Constantinople—gateway to the Middle East—Sidney Herbert, now Secretary at War, asked Florence to head up a team of nurses for the army hospital at Scutari in Turkey. Florence leapt at the chance. She arrived with a hand-picked team of thirty-eight nurses. Only fourteen had actual nursing experience; twenty-four were members of religious institutions: Roman Catholic nuns; Dissenting Deaconnesses; Protestant hospital nurses; and several Anglican sisters who had experience with cholera. Her friends Charles and Selina Bracebridge also came along as support.

Throughout the war, Florence had an uphill battle convincing the army doctors that female nurses belonged in a military hospital. But the Crimean War exposed a British military system that sent thousands of soldiers to their death from malnutrition, disease, and neglect. Sixty thousand British soldiers were sent to the Crimea. Of forty-three thousand dead, sick, or wounded—only seven thousand had been wounded by the enemy. The rest were victims of "mud, muddle, and disease."

At the end of the war, Florence Nightingale's reports and suggestions took England by storm. She became a national heroine. In 1860, the Nightingale School for Nurses opened in London with fifteen young women in the first class. Throughout her life, before she died in her sleep at the age of ninety in 1910, she worked tirelessly to institute reforms in the army regarding health and medical care.

Because, she vowed, "What happened in the Crimea must never happen again."

For Further Reading

Bull, Angela. *Florence Nightingale*. London: Hamish Hamilton, 1985.

Nolan, Jeanette C. *Florence Nightingale*. New York: Junior Literary Guild and Julian Messner, Inc., 1946.

Shore, Donna. *Florence Nightingale* (from the What Made Them Great series for young people). Englewood Cliffs, N.J.: Silver Burdett Press, a division of Simon & Shuster, Inc., 1990.

Tennyson, Alfred Lord. "Charge of the Light Brigade" (poem).

Woodham-Smith, Cecil. *Florence Nightingale*. New York: McGraw-Hill Book Company, Inc., 1951.